Blue Is
Like Blue

Praise for *Blue Is Like Blue*

'Stark and mesmerizing, these stories puzzle, disturb and seduce the reader. Shukla whittles reality down to its bare poetic core.'

– Amitabha Bagchi

'Vinod Kumar Shukla's world is set just a little bit askew and, thus, the quotidian becomes unusual, the mundane becomes remarkable. The reader is persuaded to marvel anew at the follies and foibles of the human species.'

– Arshia Sattar

'In what way is over-familiarity akin to the uncanny? In what sense are the lives we lead each day in rooms, streets, and shops not entirely our own? To find the answer to these questions, we must read the sui generis Vinod Kumar Shukla, whose work reminds us that deep originality will always finds its own home and language. His translators have taken up the questions and challenges his work poses, and these superb English versions constitute their response.'

– Amit Chaudhuri

'There's a vein of gold in Chhattisgarh and it passes under Vinod Kumar Shukla's house in Raipur. Shuklaji has been quietly mining it for the past half-century and more. The house key is encrypted, so a sensible prowler would give up and sit down with any book by this great original; these stories, deftly rendered, are an excellent place to start.'

– Irwin Allan Sealy

Blue Is Like Blue

Stories

Vinod Kumar Shukla

Translated from the Hindi
by Arvind Krishna Mehrotra
and Sara Rai

HARPERPERENNIAL

An Imprint of HarperCollins *Publishers*

HARPERPERENNIAL

First published in India by Harper Perennial 2019
An imprint of HarperCollins *Publishers*
4th Floor, Tower A, Building No. 10, DLF Cyber City,
DLF Phase II, Gurugram, Haryana – 122002
www.harpercollins.co.in

This edition published in India by Harper Perennial 2024

2 4 6 8 10 9 7 5 3 1

Grateful acknowledgement is made to the editors of *Almost Island* and *n+1*
where some of the material in this book first appeared.

P-ISBN: 978-93-5699-666-3
E-ISBN: 978-93-5302-933-3

Typeset in 11/15 Bembo Std at
Manipal Digital Systems, Manipal

Printed and bound at
Thomson Press (India) Ltd

FSC www.fsc.org
MIX
Paper from responsible sources
FSC® C010615

This book is produced from independently certified FSC® paper
to ensure responsible forest management.

For Dangudada and Ashok

contents

introduction

'THERE IS NOTHING OF me except what is here,' Vinod Kumar Shukla writes in a poem. His 'here' is a specific place: Raipur and, before that, Rajnandgaon, both cities in the tribal belt of India. They are two cities on the map, but in his imagination they are one. As he says in 'Old Veranda', 'The old veranda of our house in Rajnandgaon is now in the house in Raipur.'

Rajnandgaon is where he was born in 1937 into a family of Kanyakubja Brahmins who hailed from Uttar Pradesh, and where he had his early education. Raipur is where he taught at the Indira Gandhi Agricultural University and where he has lived for most of his working life. His subject was agricultural extension, which involved travelling to the surrounding villages to acquaint farmers with new agricultural techniques. He retired in 1996.

Shukla's meeting in 1957 with the Marxist poet Gajanan Madhav Muktibodh (1917–1964), who was then teaching in Rajnandgaon, is described in 'Old Veranda.'

The encouragement he received from the older poet, who suggested that he send his poems to a magazine whose editor he knew, proved to be decisive. Shukla's first collection was a twenty-page chapbook, *Lagbhag jaihind* (1971), the ironic title marking him out as a new voice in Hindi poetry. Some of its poems were later incorporated into his first full-length collection, the unforgettably titled *Voh aadami chala gaya naya garam coat pahankar vichar ki tarah* (1981). In the title poem, 'a blurred horse of inferior stock' is standing under a tree on a misty winter morning. A second 'blurred shape' is the horse's owner. A man 'in rubber flip-flops' is watching the scene. In the poem's last line, the man in flip-flops and the horse have changed places; the man has 'horseshoes nailed to [his] boot soles'. Marxist influence may be at work here, but only if writing about a wage earner makes one a Marxist. In the blurry images of a winter morning, the one that stands out unambiguously is the image of a workhorse superimposed on a common day labourer. Human legs appear as horse's legs.

Though there was, till the 1960s, little to distinguish Rajnandgaon and Raipur from the other wayside stations on the Howrah–Bombay rail line, in Shukla's eyes they encompass the known world. Were it left to him he would still be living in the house of his childhood:

> Ours was a family of four brothers living under one roof. The roof's shadow belonged to my youngest uncle, who was called Chachaji. He was called this at home and also outside, but wherever he was he largely kept to himself. Everyone was in awe of him. If he stepped

> out of the house more than he usually did, he came up against the world as if against a wall. He came up against it even when he was at home.
>
> ('Old Veranda')

The large family living under 'one roof' is an idea that he returns to in a poem:

> Had we all lived together
> under one roof
> without separate kitchens –
> grandfather, great aunt,
> father, uncle, siblings –
> and remained in
> the same neighbourhood…
>
> ('Had we all lived together')

By the time the poem ends, though, the family has become the human family and the 'one roof' is not of a house in Rajnandgaon but the sky. Shukla, who seldom travels and has been outside India perhaps only three or four times on literary junkets, would agree with Hazlitt that 'Foreign travel especially makes men pedants, not artists. What we seek, we must find at home or nowhere'.

In another poem, Shukla compares the flight of a bird to that of a butterfly:

> Leaving the earth,
> mounting the air,

does the bird know
that it's the earth it is leaving?
To fly above it,
you really have to go high.
And when it returns
to settle on a tree
does the bird know
that it's the earth it's returned to?
I don't have wings.
There's a small yellow butterfly
flying above the ground.

('Leaving the earth')

If the poem can be read as a metaphor for two kinds of writers, the earth-leaving bird writer and the ground-hugging butterfly writer, then Shukla clearly belongs to the latter species. In the poem, the bird doesn't know what it is distant or cut off from, or what it is returning to. Shukla's vision, by contrast, operates at street level. The people he observes and writes about wear cheap footwear and carry tattered shopping bags for their vegetables, bought in small quantities after much haggling. An early poem of his from 1960 describes a scene that will keep recurring in his fiction:

A street in the bazaar,
a busy shopper,
carrying a soiled
slightly torn bag
in each hand,

> one empty, one full.
> Inside it, potatoes, leafy
> vegetables, a garam masala
> packet, and chillies...
>
> ('A street in the bazaar')

These busy shoppers are modest, smaller-than-life people. They, in Shukla's fiction, live in rented accommodation, often in single rooms that look unfinished. The room has a window but the shutters may not have been fixed. There's a nail or peg to hang clothes from, a wall-to-wall string for the washing. When the clothes are dry, the character, always a man, places the carefully folded shirt under the pillow and, putting off the light, a single electric bulb, goes to sleep. The job of ironing the shirt is left to the weight of his warm head, as though every turn will smooth out a crease. In any case, it saves you money.

The bazaar is the place to go, especially if you have nothing to buy. As 'College' – the longest story in the book – puts it:

> Watching other shoppers was more fun than being a shopper yourself. I could spend hours in the bazaar and still leave with the same amount of money I had when I arrived. It was easy to tell who the big spenders in the crowd were. Following one of them around made you feel you'd seen everything there was to see.

The fear that you might be overcharged accompanies every transaction. Haggling is important. You have a limited amount of money but must still make your purchase:

I'd met Puttan on the way. He didn't look too happy; from his shoulder hung an empty sling bag. Puttan was in the same class as my younger brother.

'Didn't you buy anything?' I'd asked him.

'I have to get sweet limes. They're five rupees a dozen, but Father said they were four.'

'Why don't you get bananas. They're a rupee a dozen.'

'I don't have to buy bananas. I have to get sweet limes and salt.'

In the same family, the son might feel that he can haggle better than his father:

'It was nine rupees a kilo. It's clean oil,' Father said.

'If you'd waited for a day, I would have got it for eight rupees a kilo.'

'Be quiet,' Father shouted and went in. Amma followed him.

In keeping with the frugal ways of those he writes about, Shukla is a frugal storyteller. He can make, and make do, with very little. In 'The Burden', the nameless protagonist is bicycling to work when a falling leaf gets lodged in his pocket. It feels like a burden and he must stop to take it out. He stops a second time when he cannot remember if he's locked his room. It's a moment we are all familiar with, when we think we may have left something unlocked (a house, a car, a piece of luggage), or left something on, like the gas burner. Once we've made sure that this is not so, we don't think about it again. Shukla makes this forgotten moment, forgotten also because it happens so often, come alive. The man goes back to his room, and relieved to find that everything is in order he comes 'down whistling and there [is] a bounce in his step'. You begin to wonder if you are ever more surprised than when you meet yourself in the pages of a book.

A falling leaf, a passing thought, are yet substantial enough to bear the weight of narrative. One says weight, though one means lightness. 'I have tried to remove weight,' said Calvino in the first of his *Six Memos for the Next Millennium*, 'sometimes from people, sometimes from heavenly bodies, sometimes from cities; above all I have tried to remove weight from the structure of stories and from language.' But how does Shukla remove weight? 'Just as one never stops experiencing,' he has said, 'written literature is … never a completion.' Writing, for him, is 'a continuous process of becoming'. It is this quality of 'becoming', of keeping the narrative close to the minute-by-minute uncertainties of lived experience, the refusal to yoke it to a predetermined end, that gives his work its singular quality.

DRAMA CAN ARISE OUT of nothing in Shukla's stories. More often than not, it happens on a perfectly normal day, in the middle of a perfectly normal street. 'The Spare Time of the Crowd' begins with an upended empty drum that has been left by the side of a road. A man climbs up on the drum and starts shouting. Seeing a well-dressed man standing on a drum and shouting, a crowd soon gathers. The man's shoes are pinching him; he cannot walk; he doesn't know what to do. The crowd swells; there's a discussion about shoes; someone starts to cry. It's an impromptu performance and before we know it we are, as it were, glued to our seats.

You don't have to stand on a drum in the middle of a street for a crowd to collect. 'I had time on my hands,' says the narrator of 'Man in the Blue Shirt', as he observes a man carrying a pot of curd in his left hand. He then sees him going with a pot of curd in the same direction again, though he did not see him return. It is not long before someone joins him and the two start discussing this strange event: a man in a blue shirt carrying a pot of curd, who went in the same direction twice without returning from it the first time. The ordinary (someone out on an errand) is seldom, in Shukla, far from the unbelievable. It's the way he looks at the world, or the way the world comes to him. The tone, therefore, is always matter of fact, though he recognizes that his way of seeing is not everyone's. 'But I was seeing a lot more. I saw a man with two noses, a double nose,' he writes in 'Old Veranda'. 'We don't need to see anything out of the ordinary,' Robert Walser wrote in one of his stories. 'We already see so much.'

Only in the city of literature can you arrive at a street in Gudakhu Line, Rajnandgaon, and turn off into Friedrichstrasse in Berlin.

Since he sees so much, a thought in Shukla does not move to the next thought but reveals the one that is lurking behind the first or under its surface, and is for that reason unnoticed by most of us. In 'Man in the Blue Shirt', the narrator says, 'I tried to remember if I'd ever worn a blue shirt. In my mind I went over all the things at home that were blue.' The uncertain memory of wearing a blue shirt is only the beginning. The thought is like a seam that keeps unravelling and Shukla begins to see other things: 'I thought of the things in our house and their colours and made a list. My bed sheet was green and the durrie had two or three colours...' In the same story, the narrator says of his dead father, 'When he died, the watch on his wrist was still working.' After noticing the discordance between a dead man and the watch ticking on his wrist, Shukla takes the thought a step further, as though pulling at its thread: 'It's not as if I'd expected it to stop, but I did think about it.'

Discordance can sometimes take a linguistic form, through repetition, when Shukla compares a thing to itself. The effect is similar to the visual one we experience when we see a work by Bridget Riley. So, in 'Old Veranda', 'The people I met on the way were like the people one meets on the way', and in 'Man in the Blue Shirt', 'The crowd was like a crowd', 'Blue is like blue', and 'The flock of ducks looked like ducks. They had ducks' bills and feathers'. The repetition and the resultant discordance gains in effect if one also remembers that Shukla is sometimes repeating an image that we have previously encountered in his poems:

> There were many flocks of ducks,
> looking like flocks of men.

This flock of ducks
was like a duck.
It had a duck's bill and wings.

('To a friend I said')

It is not only thoughts hidden behind other thoughts that Shukla reveals. His characters have hidden sides to them. They act in unpredictable ways and do the opposite of what we expect them to do. It takes the reader by surprise as much as it does the characters themselves. This is true of two stories in particular, 'The Man's Woman' and 'Shoe Ashtray'.

Strange things happen in Shukla's fiction: a heron enters a college classroom and turns back when it sees there's a lecture going on; a father's dentures become his sons' inheritance, the upper one going to the older son and the lower one to the younger; in the cinema theatre, 'Urine from the women's toilet would spill out and after passing the first-class and second-class seats, reach the front of the hall...' The utterly mundane and the humdrum are constantly being transformed into the unexpected and the marvellous. In the mundane lies also the possibility of happiness: 'It was a matter of great joy that people would set out to buy okra and would return home after having bought okra.'

In the provincial world that he creates in extraordinary detail, everything is within the realm of the possible. In it, the quotidian folds into the comic, the real into the imagined. The heron did turn back from the classroom, the son did think of the father's dentures as inheritance, the urine did travel down the cinema theatre, and perhaps the man did have two noses, one for each of his two selves. In Shukla's own words, 'I believe that those who feel fantasy is unnecessary are mistaken. Without it, reality can never be revealed.' It's a statement that neither Walser nor his early admirer Franz Kafka would have disagreed with.

At the Jaipur Literature Festival 2011, Vinod Kumar Shukla asked Sara Rai why were there so many people standing in line, each clutching a book. Told that they were all waiting to have their books signed by J.M. Coetzee, he looked puzzled. Hindi writers sign books, but privately, and seldom is there a line of people waiting for them to do so. Moreover, the name Coetzee meant nothing to him, nor did the names of the other world writers present on the occasion. One explanation for it could be that he reads only in Hindi, which perhaps has more speakers than Mandarin Chinese but in which little gets translated. Even if it did, you doubt whether Shukla would be interested. Recently, when asked in an email if he was familiar with any European writers, for it is they who often come to mind when you read him, Shukla did not evade the question. He simply ignored it. The question did not deserve an answer. Just as the flock of ducks looks like ducks, we might say that Shukla looks only like himself, like Shukla. If there are any influences, it's the one that he touches on in 'Old Veranda' and reiterates in an interview:

> My mother possibly took a month's break after my birth from watching films, so I always say that I have had a month more of life and a month less of films. Watching films was not considered such a bad thing

> then, so it was not uncommon to find someone at home humming a movie tune, or standing at the window to catch strains of the dialogue. The posters were a huge novelty though. We would beg the men who came to paste them on walls to put some up on our walls too … But by then, we were quite adept at this double life, at how quickly we could slip out from the fantastic worlds of Sitara Devi and Fearless Nadia into the mundane everydayness of our homes. In fact, I think that's one of the reasons why I don't think in linguistic terms. My work comes to me visually.

Shukla must be among the few writers alive whose work has appeared in journals where world literature is published or discussed – *Granta*, *Metamorphoses*, *Modern Poetry in Translation*, *Some Kind of Beautiful Signal*, *The Baffler*, *n+1* – but who has heard neither of these journals nor of world literature. In contrast to his unawareness of the term and his indifference to the subjects that keep the assembly line of global fiction moving (historical trauma, acts of terrorism, personal turmoil), is the attention he lavishes on the fleeting observations, thoughts, memories and gestures that for most of us, regardless of where we live, constitute our lives. To read him is to read not a fictionalized version of what is already stencilled on the wall, but what is constantly being inscribed in and erased from the margins of our consciousness.

Arvind Krishna Mehrotra & Sara Rai

twenty rupees

HE HAD LOST TWENTY rupees. After he'd looked everywhere and couldn't find them, he had his meal and went to sleep. It was afternoon.

When he woke it was evening. It felt like morning to him. It was only later that he realized it was evening. Immediately afterwards he remembered that he'd lost twenty rupees. He found it odd that it wasn't the first thing that came to him when he woke. He lay there with his eyes shut and did not open them for some time. It had grown dark. For no reason in particular it occurred to him that this time of day could be mistaken for five in the morning, and that inside the room there was little difference between morning light and evening light.

He was lying under a sheet and was drenched in sweat. However hot it may be, he could not sleep unless he had bolted the door and pulled up the sheet. It was an old habit of his. As he lay there, he could feel the perspiration trickling down his brow. He did not want it to get into his ear. He quickly released his hand from under the sheet and passed it over his forehead. The tips of his fingers, when he looked at them, were wet. He raised himself on his elbow and saw that the depression on the pillow made by his head was damp. Out of curiosity, he leaned forward and checked the sheet at the foot of the bed. There were sweat marks there too. He still did not want to get up. He pulled up the sheet and lay down again. He looked at the door. It was bolted and the paint was peeling off. When he kept looking at the door, he felt that instead of the door there was a ten-rupee note stretched on it, covering it from top to bottom. If he tried to go out of the door the note would get torn. He knew the sound that paper makes when it tears, but not the sound of paper money tearing. He'd never heard it. If currency notes got torn, he thought, they could still be used, so long as the serial numbers were intact.

He gave his head a jerk and got up. He always felt restless if he slept during the day. It was different on holidays, for then he wanted to sleep after a meal. He felt like a bath and quickly came out of the room with his soap and towel. The bathroom was filthy. There were many tenants with their families living in the area and some of them used the bathroom. Nothing stayed clean for very long. Then he remembered that he'd left his room open. He usually left it open even if he went out for half an hour, but today he went back and locked it.

The overhead storage tanks had received the sun all day and the water in the tap was almost boiling. He turned on the tap and let the water run for a while. There were small pieces of blue detergent soap lying on the floor, and in a corner a little girl's dirty printed panties. With the thumb and forefinger of his left hand he lifted the panties, then flung them out of the door. They landed on the stairs with a squelch. He was filled with revulsion. He washed his hands thoroughly with soap.

The rent for his room was eight rupees a month, which was all he could afford. Had he been able to afford more he'd have left it long ago and gone somewhere else. His salary was only ninety rupees. His neighbour worked in the municipality and had white patches on his hands and feet. When this neighbour went past him, he'd hold his breath so that he wouldn't inhale the germs. He'd been working as a clerk for only two months, having taken up the job immediately after matriculation. His home town was forty-five miles away.

The tap was still running. He scrubbed the bathroom floor with his feet. By then the water from the tap had cooled a little. As he bathed, he thought he should spend a little more time searching for the twenty rupees. If you do things in a hurry it is easy to make a mistake and overlook something.

He finished his bath and came back to the room. As soon as he entered it he bolted the door. He bolted it at the top, then at the bottom, which was unnecessary. The door would have been secure even if he hadn't bolted it at the bottom.

The room was in a mess. While searching for the twenty rupees in the morning he had turned it upside down. There were clothes and books strewn all over. The khaki trousers that he was going to wear again that day were lying in a corner. He washed his own clothes, rather than give them to the dhobi. He believed that they lasted longer if you washed them yourself. Picking up the trousers, he thought that he should be ironing his clothes too. This way he could save the money he spent on getting them ironed. The shirt he'd hung out on the line was dry now. He folded it carefully and put it under the pillow. Then he took out an old leather pouch from the suitcase and sat down on the bed. His mother had given him the pouch. He sent his father fifty rupees every month. He had three brothers, all younger than him. One was in class nine and another in class one. Both went to an English-medium school. The youngest, in a Hindi-medium school, was in class two. His father was headmaster in an elementary school. He thought he'd study for a BA and take the exam as an external student. He wanted his younger brothers to get a good education.

His mother would say only fools feel sad if they lose something. What was lost was lost. He decided not to think about it any more. His father though would be angry if he heard that he'd lost so much money. Once he got a beating just because he'd lost two annas. This month he wouldn't be able to send home fifty rupees; he'd send only forty. He began to calculate how to make up the twenty rupees he'd lost. He went to the cinema once a week. He'd sacrifice going to the cinema. He paid twenty rupees a month to the eatery where he had his meals. He wouldn't eat there on Sundays and save some money. He'd give up his evening tea. He'd live like a miser and wouldn't spend any money unless absolutely necessary.

He changed his clothes and thought he should go for a walk. He felt like eating a kulfi when he passed the kulfi seller's stall, but he resisted the temptation. He noticed a couple of crumpled pieces of paper lying on the road that normally he would have kicked aside. He remembered that once while returning from office he'd seen a silver rupee coin. He had stopped and tried to pick up the coin but it remained stuck to the road, to the merriment of some boys sitting at the roadside paan shop. Later, he found out that when the tar on the road melted in the heat, boys out for some fun would press a coin into it. By evening the coin would be stuck fast.

On the way back, he found the kulfi seller still sitting there and again he felt like eating a kulfi. It was only a question of two annas, but wasn't that how he ended up spending a lot of money? He did not eat the kulfi.

The next day he sent a money order to his father along with a note:

> Respected Father, I touch your feet. It pains me to tell you that I have lost twenty rupees. I am sending only forty rupees this month. I hope you will forgive me. I touch respected Amma's feet. Your devoted son, Mannan.

There were tears in his eyes when he wrote this.

Three days later, while sending a money order of ten rupees to his father, he wrote in his tiny handwriting:

> Respected Father, I touch your feet. You will be pleased to know that I have found the twenty rupees. I'd kept them in a pocket of the suitcase where I usually keep letters, and they were meant to pay the eatery where I take my meals. I am sending you the ten rupees that were short. I touch respected Amma's feet. Your devoted son, Mannan.

He found there was a crowd outside the cinema hall that night. The tickets for ten annas were being sold in the black market for a rupee. He thought he may as well watch the show, now that he'd come all the way. He bought the ten anna ticket for a rupee and entered the hall.

1964

the burden

HE'D HAD HIS BREAKFAST and was back home. No sooner was he back than he changed into his office clothes and put on his shoes. He oiled and combed his hair. He picked up the bicycle keys and the lock to put on the door. The cycle was on the veranda, from where he wheeled it out and started for office. This was his daily routine; he went through it without thinking about it twice.

He was going at a good speed even though he had plenty of time. The road ran along Phoolbagh. It took him roughly twenty minutes to reach his office. It was summer and the dry leaves of the neem trees that lined either side of the road were constantly falling. One of the leaves got lodged in his pocket. He found this odd. He continued to pedal, and as he did so he put his left hand inside the pocket and tried to take out the leaf, but it crumbled and stuck to the cloth. He stopped the bike and turned out the pocket to clean it. The leaf fragments in his pocket could hardly be called heavy nor did he have to stop to remove them, but stop he did.

He had reached Phoolbagh when it struck him that he might have forgotten to lock his room. He tried hard to remember but a nagging doubt still remained. Yesterday the same thing had happened. He'd come halfway when he'd had to turn back. He wanted to make sure the lock was secure.

He pulled at it and found that it was. Having made certain, he went to office with an easy mind.

He'd been paid two days ago. He had just one bed in his room and a trunk that he never locked, though he often thought that he should get one for it. He had kept his salary in the trunk, inside the pocket of a freshly washed shirt. He'd then placed a handkerchief over the pocket to keep the money from falling out if the clothes were moved around. Perhaps he also thought that the handkerchief would conceal the money, make it less noticeable.

He lived in a rented room behind Lashkar Hotel. Bhagwat, who worked for the hotel, would come round to sweep the rooms, starting with the ones on the left. He didn't think twice before entering a room even if no one was there. Several times it happened that Bhagwat had come to sweep the room while he was bathing in the common facility. He'd hurried through the bath and returned quickly to the room. He didn't want Bhagwat to be there in his absence. He didn't trust these hotel employees one bit, though so far he'd had no complaints.

He thought he had probably locked his room, but what if he hadn't? He felt annoyed with himself for being unsure. He could still go back and check. This time he felt certain that he'd forgotten to lock it. His entire salary was in the trunk and he did not want to take a chance. If he went back, the extra pedalling might tire him out but at least the money would be safe. In any case, he was early for office. Even if he went back to the room to make sure, he wouldn't get late. Should he or should he not, he asked himself. Without being aware of what he was doing, he slowed down. He went round the traffic island at the same slow speed, and then, pedalling furiously, returned to his room. He almost collided with a cart loaded with a slab of ice but managed to avoid it at the last minute.

He saw Bhagwat standing on the veranda as he approached the hotel. He didn't like this at all. He locked the bike and went up to his room. From the expression on his face and by his walk, he wanted to convey to Bhagwat that he was in a hurry and had forgotten something. While climbing the stairs he turned round to look. Bhagwat was watching him. Oh shit! Hope the bastard hasn't caught on, he thought. On reaching the room he paused and looked behind him again. Bhagwat wasn't there. He pulled at the lock and found that it was fastened. He came down whistling and there was a bounce in his step. He asked the pandit who was the hotel cook for a glass of water and then for another; he was thirsty. He left for office after drinking two glasses of water.

He felt light-hearted. He stopped the bike at a restaurant that he passed and looked at the clock on the wall. It was not yet eleven; he still had plenty of time. He'd been wise, he thought, to go back to his room and reassure himself about the lock. If he hadn't, he'd have been thinking about it all the time he was at work. These things do happen. After all, anyone can make a mistake, and the same mistake can be repeated. He could have lost the 150 rupees, his entire salary. How then would he have paid last month's bills and met this month's expenses? He may even have had to give up his room. He'd done the right thing, he told himself.

In fact, what he had feared had happened once before. The lock he had at the time was a press lock. He'd gone out for a stroll in the evening, and half an hour later when he returned he found the lock hanging open. He'd forgotten to press the shank. It had got him worried but his things were safe.

He worked with a relaxed mind and came home in the evening. He unlocked the door. He was extremely tired. The moment he lay down he felt sleepy. He closed his eyes and turned over on his side. It felt good to stretch his arms and legs. His daily round to the office and back required a lot of cycling and his legs felt heavy, as though he'd climbed several flights of stairs to reach his room. After a while he got up and opened the trunk. He took out all the money that was in the shirt pocket and went down to pay off his debts. He paid for the previous month's food and the rent. Then he handed Bhagwat a fiver to give to the dhobi. He was out of oil, soap and toothpaste, which he bought from the corner shop. He possessed just two handkerchiefs and purchased another. For the past month he'd been wondering if he should buy two more banians and this time he thought he would. He needed to buy chappals too, for he had just the one pair of shoes, but with only eight rupees and a few annas left to last him the whole month, he decided not to. He'd have bought them if he had some more money. He carried the stuff back to his room.

The next morning, before setting out for office, he wore his new banian and changed the set of clothes he was wearing. In his pocket was the new handkerchief. He combed his hair and put on his shoes, then picked up the bicycle keys and the lock.

He'd only gone a short distance when the faint misgiving obscurely entered his mind that he'd forgotten to lock the room. He smiled and shook his head, then continued to go along at the same speed. If someone had then seen him smiling to himself they'd have been surprised. There were neem trees on either side of the road. It was summer and hundreds of dry leaves were falling, but not one found its way into his pocket. He carried on cycling, without stopping or slowing down.

1963

fish

WE RAN INTO A narrow lane. Our house was close by. The roads were full of people; it was the day of the weekly bazaar. Then it started to rain and the crowd dispersed rapidly.

We were running because we were afraid that without water the fish might die while they were still in the bag. There were three fish in it. One had died while Father was buying them. Two were alive. I could feel them agitating in the bag. I thought I'd ask Father for one of them and release it into the well. We'd watch it become really big. If we wanted to play with the fish we could take it out in a bucket and put it back when we'd finished playing.

It had begun to rain hard. I stood in the downpour and opened the bag to the sky so that rain would fall on the fish. It might help them revive. Santu had gone and stood under a ledge to keep from getting wet. Still, we were both soaked to the skin. Just then, perhaps sensing in the raindrops a pond or river nearby, one of the fish made a big leap. The bag almost fell from my hands.

We'd shut ourselves inside the bathroom. The bucket was full, so we emptied out half and put the three fish in the water. Had the bucket been full they would have jumped out. Once, a small fish that I'd been holding had slipped from my hand and disappeared into the bathroom drain. Santu and I were immediately on our knees, trying to find it. When we couldn't we went to the spot behind the house where our drain met a bigger drain. But we couldn't see the fish there either. Didi, our elder sister, said that from there the fish would have made it to the biggest drain of the city and eventually reached the Mohara River, which was three miles away.

Santu shivered in the cold. We'd get a beating if Ma saw us wet. I told Santu he'd better wring his shirt. Both of us took off our shirts and wrung them. Then we tried to get the water out of our pants by kneading them with our fists. Wearing just the pants and holding our wet shirts, we sat around the bucket. The fish right at the bottom was the one that had died.

'We'll ask Father for the one that's on top,' I said to Santu.

Santu nodded and said, 'Okay.' He was gazing lovingly at the fish. He would have liked to touch them but was too scared. I moved closer to the bucket and, catching hold of the fish, I said, 'Go on, Santu, touch it!'

'No, it will bite,' he said, refusing.

'See, I'm touching it and it's not biting, is it? This fish doesn't bite. Here, touch it!'

Santu hesitantly put a finger on the fish. Then he got frightened and pulled his hand away.

'Come, what are you scared of?' I said, picking up one of the two fish.

It kept slipping from my hand so I put it back into the bucket. It leapt up as soon as it was in the water, splashing some of it on us. Santu stepped back, startled.

I wanted to see my reflection in the eyes of the fish that had died. Didi said that you can't see yourself in the eyes of a dead fish.

I dipped my hand into the bucket and took out the fish that looked like it was dead. I laid it gently on the bathroom floor. I shook it by the tail a few times but it did not move at all. It's single-haired long moustache was curled at the ends.

'Look into its eye, Santu. Can you see yourself?'

Santu was sitting at a safe distance because the fish was now on the floor, out of the bucket. When I said that, he moved a little closer, eagerly peering into the fish's eye.

'Go closer,' I said. 'Can you see it? Didi says you can't see your reflection in the eyes of a dead fish.'

Santu kept sitting there quietly, his head bent, looking into the eye of the fish but not saying whether he could see his reflection or not.

'It's no good asking you,' I said, catching the fish in both hands. I brought it very close to my face and saw a dim shadow in its eyes. I couldn't tell if it was my reflection that I saw or whether this was what the colour of the eyes had become.

'It might still be alive. Go quietly and bring Didi here,' I said to Santu. And I put the fish back into the bucket.

Santu came back and said, 'Didi's asleep.'

'She's sleeping now, in the middle of the morning?' I asked, surprised. 'Where's Ma?'

'She's grinding spices.'

My heart sank. 'That's terrible. She must be grinding them for the fish. It means they're going to cook them today,' I said sadly.

'So, will they soon cut them into pieces?' asked Santu innocently.

'Yes.'

That made Santu sad too.

A wooden board in the house had been kept aside for this purpose. There was a zigzag of knife marks on it. The board used to be kept behind the storage barrel on the veranda and would be taken out the day there was fish to be cooked. Chopping the fish was the servant's job. It had stopped raining. I came out into the courtyard and saw that the board had been washed and kept ready. There was some ash from the stove lying near it. I figured Bhaggu must be at the well, sharpening the knife. The door of the bathroom was open and I could see the bucket with the fish in it. Ma wasn't around. She might have been upstairs. She didn't like fish or meat being cooked in the house. Father had hoped that we children would take to eating meat, but Ma had strictly forbidden us to do so. And it wasn't as if we wanted to either. So it was only Father who ate it.

Bhaggu seemed to know that the fish were in the bathroom. He went there at once and brought them out wrapped in his angocha. Our enthusiasm for nurturing fishes in the well had died somewhat. Father still wasn't home. I went into the room and found Didi there, lying on her side. I beckoned to Santu to come in and change out of his wet clothes. He must have made a sound while doing so, for Didi turned round and saw us. She wasn't pleased to see how wet our clothes were, but she spoke kindly to us. She dressed Santu nicely, in ironed clothes, though we didn't know why she'd done that. Just as I was going to put on the clothes that had been washed at home, she told me to wear the ones that had come from the dhobi. She took them out for me from the tin trunk. Santu had long hair, so it was still wet. Didi wiped his hair with a towel and oiled it. She held his chin with her left hand when she combed his hair. Santu kept his large eyes fixed on Didi all the while. Everyone said that Didi was very pretty.

'Didi,' I said, 'there's fish being cooked today. There were three of them but I think one is already dead. Bhaggu's going to cut them just now.' Didi said nothing at first, but then she asked me to close the door from outside when we went out of the room. She wanted to be by herself. She didn't feel well. Santu and I came out of the room quietly. I could see Didi lying down as I shut the door.

We were standing against the pillar behind Bhaggu, watching the fish being cut. Bhaggu first picked up one of the fish and hit it a couple of times against a stone. He rubbed ash all over the fish, and now it looked as if it was really dead. He then placed it on the board and with a quick movement chopped off the head. The fish did not agitate at all. Just then Santu grabbed one fish and ran out. Bhaggu left the fish he'd been cutting and chased him, 'Hey! Hey! Hey!' I kept standing there. The headless fish that had been rubbed with ash was lying on the board and I noticed that the third fish that was still wrapped in the angocha quivered once. Santu's run off with the dead fish, I thought.

It seemed to me that I could hear Didi quietly sobbing in her room. I opened the door as slowly as I could and went in to find Didi lying on her side, with the sari pulled over her face, weeping. With each sob, a shudder would go through her body. I remembered the twitching of the fish under the angocha. I closed the door and came out. Bhaggu and Santu weren't back yet. I came to the courtyard and saw that Santu was near the well, lying flat on his stomach. He was holding the fish with both hands and hiding it under him. Bhaggu was doing his best to snatch it away. He might have been worried that if Santu managed to throw the fish into the well, he'd hear no end of it from Father. I could hear Father yelling at the top of his voice from somewhere inside.

THE THREE FISH HAD been chopped into several pieces and the area around the board was strewn with shiny round scales. The door to the room where Didi had been lying was open. Ma was inside. Father was walking up and down. He looked angry. Didi was sobbing louder than before. I got the feeling that Father had beaten her.

Just as Bhaggu was leaving, Father said to him so that everyone could hear, 'Bhaggu! Next time that Romeo Naren comes anywhere near this house, make sure you break his limbs and throw him out. I'll handle the rest.'

Bhaggu nodded and left. Santu was standing there, very quiet. His clean clothes had got muddied, and his hair that had been combed so lovingly by Didi was full of dirt.

When I went into the bathroom, I got the smell of fish. I sat down beside the bucket and swirled the water around with my hand. Then I upended the bucket and for a moment the water filled the bathroom drain, but soon the drain was quite empty. The smell of fish seemed to fill the whole house.

1957–58

man in the blue shirt

I HAD TIME ON my hands.

Standing by the road I saw people going past, though there was no one in particular that I was looking at. After a while I thought I should pick one person to focus on.

There was a man in a blue shirt. He was holding a pot of curd and I saw him turn towards Gudakhu Line. I noticed him. The pot of curd was in his left hand and he was wearing glasses. I saw him clearly; I did. The crowd was like a crowd.

Soon afterwards I saw him a second time, carrying a pot of curd. He was coming from the same direction as before and turned towards Gudakhu Line. I hadn't seen him returning from there. You can't go to the same place twice without returning from it once. I was sure it was the same man. I noticed his trousers, his long nose, and his chappals that I hadn't noticed earlier. It's not that he'd worn nothing below the waist the first time I saw him. His nose too must have been long, the same as it was now, though he could have been wearing shoes instead of chappals. But he still had a pot of curd in his left hand. This was important. After all, it could have been in his right hand. I should have had someone with me, for then we could both have looked at the man in the blue shirt and compared notes. I thought that if I were to continue standing there I'd see him again, going towards Gudakhu Line with a pot of curd, though he wouldn't return from there even once. I could be friends with the man in the blue shirt.

There was an old man standing a little ahead of me on the same side of the road. There was no one on the other side. I recognized my neighbour. He wasn't fat. I said, 'Did you see the man in the blue shirt going towards Gudakhu Line? He went there twice but he didn't return the first time. Both times he was holding a pot of curd. His nose was long and he wore glasses.'

A boy of about ten came and stood near the old man. Two women soon joined them. I started walking with them though my house was in the opposite direction. I told them about the man in the blue shirt and we began to discuss him.

'How old do you think he was?' asked the old man.

'He wore glasses and had a long nose. He wore chappals. Couldn't have been younger than me.'

'It must be Shankar Dutt. He lives near Gudakhu Line.'

'But Shankar Dutt wouldn't have a blue shirt,' the younger woman said.

'He must have had a new one stitched. It's not that Shankar Dutt can't wear a blue shirt.'

'Was the shirt new?' the boy asked me.

'I didn't notice.'

'The curd must have fallen short the first time and he came back to get more, but you may not have noticed him. You only saw him when he was going back with the curd. Something like that must have happened,' said the older woman.

'He could have changed the shirt if he'd wanted to,' said the boy.

This time I noticed that the boy's face was yellow. He annoyed me.

'No one changes their shirt every minute. The same shirt can be worn for two or three days,' the older woman said irritably.

The boy turned round and started walking behind us. He tried to trip the older woman by stepping on her chappal. She seemed to be unaware of this. He was walking with his head bowed and hands held together at the back. The boy's face resembled the woman's.

Finally I saw the man in blue returning from Gudakhu Line. That was something to be pleased about.

'There he comes,' I said. 'You can look at him now.'

'Where is he?' asked the boy, almost pushing me aside.

'It's not Shankar Dutt,' the old man said to the younger woman.

'His nose isn't long,' said the older one.

The old man waved out to the man in blue. We didn't approve of this, the two women and I. The boy may have liked the gesture. The man in the blue shirt was taken aback; he looked busy and tired.

'This shirt is old,' said the old man, feeling the blue shirt. The boy and I also felt it. The two women had moved away and were not looking at us. A dog began to growl at them so they came back.

'I don't know you,' said the man in the blue shirt, looking up at the sky in distress.

I said, 'Please don't get angry. My father died about three weeks ago. Twice I saw you going towards Gudakhu Line holding a pot of curd but I didn't see you coming back from there. It's only now that I've seen you returning. I'm happy to see you. So are we all.'

'Well, I've gone past this spot a few times and come back the same way but you didn't see me. And it's only now that I've noticed how white your shirt is. I have to go now, to buy some more curd.' He was still irritated.

'Why do you need to buy so much curd?' asked the younger woman.

'I don't know. First it was my wife who wanted some, then it was my mother. Now it's my wife again. My mother and wife live together and there's no one other than me to run errands. I'm sorry to hear about his father. Mine died when I was still young.'

Out of respect, he did not look at the women directly when he spoke.

'I hope you'll pardon us,' I said.

'You look like Shankar Dutt from a distance,' the boy said loudly.

'Shankar Dutt is my younger son's friend. They've known each other since they were kids,' the old man said.

'Are you expecting guests?'

'What's your name?'

'Shankar Dutt doesn't have a blue shirt.'

'Well, he might have acquired one recently,' the old man said, making a face. 'Shankar Dutt has a long nose.'

The man in the blue shirt left in a hurry.

'Your shirt isn't really white,' the old man said to me as we started walking.

I tried to remember if I'd ever worn a blue shirt. In my mind I went over all the things at home that were blue. The sky isn't particularly blue. Blue is like blue. A group of boys strolled past wearing clothes that were of five different colours. We came across an ochre-coloured house in Gudakhu Line. The old men wore dirty white shirts.

The saris the two women wore were colourful and the boy's pants were khaki. Most people like many colours and are not very choosy. I thought of the things in our house and their colours and made a list. My bed sheet was green and the durrie had two or three colours. I was certain that one of them was red and the other green. The bottle of pills for stomach ache had a red cap and the towel had white and green stripes. There was a white enamel mug with a blue handle on the windowsill. My pen was brown and the cover of the book on my bed was blue and pink. The letters in it were black. My brother and his wife, my sister, my mother, and particularly my father owned several things that were in different colours, but I did not dwell on them. There were other things in our house that I thought about. The ink was purple and the bar of soap was red. The travel bag was brown, and with some effort I remembered a green tumbler. Not that it was anything special. Emeralds are green. I felt as if I was conducting a search. I was hungry.

Everyone had moved on ahead of me. I walked fast and caught up with them. I explained to the old man, 'I started thinking about colours because I wanted to take my mind off my father's death. I think you know my elder brother. I don't get along with my sister-in-law.'

When we'd walked ahead of the others, the old man said slowly, 'Neither do I with my daughters-in-law. Your sister-in-law must have been happy when your father died. I'm sure my daughters-in-law are looking forward to mine.'

We'd walked ahead of them on purpose. He'd turn round occasionally to look behind him, and when we both turned round we saw three buffaloes running in our direction. We stepped aside quickly. 'We won't tell my daughters-in-law,' said the old man in a whisper. The three buffaloes came very close to the women, raising a lot of dust and almost knocking them over. The women started walking alongside us. They looked frightened.

'Where has the boy gone?' I asked.

'He must have gone home,' said the old man, smiling.

'What was it you were thinking about colours?' the younger woman asked me.

The older woman gave the old man an angry look. He said nothing. He had a serious expression on his face.

'Did you see the buffaloes coming?' she asked me. 'You kept looking back and you moved to one side of the road.'

'Blue is like blue,' I said to the younger woman. 'Blue is like blue,' I said again, a little louder than before. I thought no one had heard me the first time.

'We've reached the grocer's,' said the old man drily. The two women went into the crowded shop.

'I won't get the money to buy tobacco,' the old man said to me.

'Who gives you the money?'

'The older one. But I've hidden away a whole lot of tobacco. No one at home knows about it. It's not that I love hoarding tobacco but I won't let these people harass me. My older son doesn't like me at all and the younger one's the same, but I'm not going to die anytime soon. I broke my right hand fourteen months ago.' He opened and closed his right fist a few times to show me. His hand was crooked near the wrist.

'Looking at it, no one could say that your hand was broken. My father was fifty-five when he died,' I said.

'I'll stay here. You go ask my elder daughter-in-law to give you a rupee for my tobacco,' the old man said to me.

I went into the crowded shop and said to her, 'He wants a rupee for tobacco.'

'What kind does he buy?'

'Leaf tobacco, I think.'

'A whole rupee for leaf tobacco!' she said, giving me the money from her purse. The old man was standing on one side, watching us. I gave him the rupee.

'I don't trust my sons,' he said.

'I miss my father,' I said.

'What was she saying when she gave you the rupee?' asked the old man.

'How much tobacco have you put away?' I asked.

'Three large shopping bags. All full.'

'What will you do with so much tobacco?'

'I've been saving it for four years.'

'Why do you keep saving tobacco? Isn't it better to save money instead? You can then buy tobacco whenever you need to. And the money can be used for other things as well.'

'I get tea twice a day,' the old man said.

'The elder daughter-in-law,' he went on, 'has the habit of going through my coat pockets. I find the coat useful in winter. The rest of the time I use it like a suitcase to put my things in. It has many pockets and they can hold a lot. It also has two secret pockets. In one of them I've kept a ten-rupee note and in the other I've kept two ten-rupee notes. In one of the large pockets I've kept a new safety razor blade with the wrapper removed, just in case. I cannot keep a dog to guard the coat, not that I like dogs anyway. My daughter-in-law might cut her finger if she searches the big pocket. I once put my hand in a pocket and there was a sharp pin in it that pricked me. I've no idea how it came to be there. I'll let you know if she cuts her finger. The bags of tobacco are easy to hide in the woodshed. Up ahead in a lane on the right is a sweetmeat seller. His jalebis are excellent. On Mondays and Thursdays I pretend I'm going for my morning walk but go and have the jalebis. At the end of that lane is an eatery. The kachauri and dahi aloo there are first rate. Once every two or three months I go there too, after telling them at home that I have an upset stomach and am skipping a meal. There's a patch of ringworm on my neck. You can't see it because it's hidden by my collar but at night it itches real bad.'

'So you wear your suitcase in winter,' I joked.

'You should put a patch of ringworm in the pocket of your coat,' I said mischievously, turning my face away.

'What do you keep in the other pockets?' I asked.

The old man asked, 'Did your father never hoard tobacco or anything like it?'

'No,' I said, 'I don't think so, though he did chew it sometimes. What I do know is that he had three pairs of glasses. Two of them are broken but one is okay. To get so many glasses made would have cost him a lot. When he died, the watch on his wrist was still working. It's not as if I'd expected it to stop, but I did think about it. My elder brother has it now. If I get the chance I'll show it to you. My mother and brother were always getting angry with him. They had a difficult life because he never made much money.'

The old man went on, 'The other pockets of the coat are stuffed with old newspaper clippings. One day I'll sort them out and throw away the ones I don't need. A few days ago I tore up some of them, and day before yesterday I tore two more from the ones I'd saved. In 1955 I'd written an apology to a government official asking pardon for having been rude to him. I didn't mean to be rude. Copies of the letter are still with me. I'll tear them up now. I can't make up my mind about what to keep in the pockets. There's a safety razor blade sharpener made of glass on the windowsill. It won't break and can go into one of the pockets. So can a glass tumbler. Safety razor blades are something your father could have collected. Any idea what else I should keep in the coat?'

'Postcards and envelopes,' I suggested.

'There's a shirt button and the stub of a pencil,' said the old man.

'You can keep keys in the pocket too.'

'I don't use keys because anything that I need to put away safely is already in the coat. I leave it unbuttoned. The money is in the secret pocket.'

'Can you open and close your right fist again and show me?' I said to him.

The old man shifted the rupee he was holding in his right hand to the left, and I watched him as he opened and closed his right fist.

'It's hard to tell that your hand was broken,' I said, expressing surprise.

'I can see my elder brother coming,' I said, turning away in the opposite direction. 'Has he gone?' I asked, still looking away. The old man said nothing. This was because another man had come and stood there in his place without my noticing. My brother was gone. I saw the two women coming back with the old man.

'I don't know your elder brother,' said the man who was there instead of the old man.

'He has a shaven head,' I said, staring at the man's yellow shirt. The flock of ducks looked like ducks. They had ducks' bills and feathers. The ducks were walking on the road and they'd step away to one side when a cycle or car came along. They were headed for the market. Everyone seemed to be going to Gudakhu Line; something must have happened there. When I passed my hand over my shaven head I felt as if I was feeling my unshaven chin. I imagined the old man combing my hair with his right hand, parting it on the right side. And the man in the blue shirt had become friends with me. The next thing I imagined was that all of us, the man in the blue shirt, the old man, the boy and I went to Gudakhu Line holding the pot of curd. I didn't like the man in the yellow shirt who'd come and stood there in the old man's place.

I did not want to imagine anything else.

1971

piece of gold

I WAS STANDING ON the roof. I should not have been standing there. It had started to drizzle. There was a crowd on the street below. The crowd began to scatter as soon as the rain became heavy. To keep from getting wet, people took shelter inside shops and on the verandas of houses. A young man of nineteen or twenty was walking in the middle of the street. He seemed to be in no great hurry. It was Binesh. I was surprised that he had allowed himself to get wet. It didn't seem to bother him that this clothes were completely soaked, though usually he was particular about them. I stood close to a wall to save myself from the rain. The wall was part of a room that the landlord had started building but then he had changed his mind.

I came down from the roof and waited for Binesh. It was raining so hard that anyone else would have made a run for it and taken shelter on the veranda.

'Why are you getting wet?' The water that had collected on the roof was falling on the corrugated tin awning. The sound of the rain was loud, so I had to yell to be heard.

Binesh did not reply but came and joined me on the veranda. His wet shirt was sticking to his chest, the banian under it clearly visible. His trousers were soaked and their cuffs spattered with mud. The spot where he stood had become wet. When we came inside, he went to a corner of the room. He stood there shivering. My unwashed pajama and shirt were hanging on a peg. I'd been wearing them for a week and thought I would take out a fresh set to wear the next day. I gave him the unwashed shirt and pajama and told him to get out of his wet clothes. When he took off his shirt I saw that his banian was torn at both shoulders. He changed his clothes. I hung his shirt and the banian on the clothesline in the room. When I picked up the trousers he stopped me from doing so. He hung them up himself.

It was morning. The room was dark because of the rain. It was still raining hard. Binesh put on my clothes and sat down next to me on the bed. The bed was against a wall that now served as our backrest. A part of the wall was damp and I thought there must be a crack in it somewhere.

Binesh got up. He went to the clothesline and put his hand inside his trouser pocket. He took out something and brought it to me in his clenched fist. I raised my head to look at him. He was buttoning his shirt. Binesh had hair sprouting on his chin but hadn't yet started shaving or trimming it. I once offered to trim it for him, but he twisted away the hand in which I held the scissors.

'I want to tell you something.' I didn't like the way he came and stood right in front of me. He had spoken in a whisper and I wondered what he was going to say.

'Is it something special?'

'Yes, it is. You won't tell anyone, will you?'

'I won't. What is it?'

He opened his fist. There was a piece of metal in it, the colour of gold, but before I could take a proper look he closed his fist again. It was a solid-looking piece, as though bits of gold ornaments had been melted down to make it.

'What is it?' I asked.

'Looks like gold, doesn't it?' Binesh said.

Binesh's forehead was wet. I could not decide if they were beads of sweat or he hadn't dried his hair properly.

'It could be brass,' I said.

'Not really.' He sat down next to me and opened his fist. From its colour, the piece of metal looked like pure gold. I held out my hand and he put the piece in it. As soon as I held it I realized how heavy it was. I had not expected it to be so heavy. I closed my fist. The piece of metal was warm from being in contact with Binesh's body. I gave it back to him.

'Well, it does look like gold,' I said.

'I hope you did not steal it,' I said, smiling at him nervously, as if he had committed a crime that I had been hesitating to bring up.

He got up from the bed and went to the door to look at the rain. Then he shut the door. I did not like what he did.

'Why did you shut the door?'

'For no particular reason,' Binesh said.

'It's hot in here. At least there was some light coming in from outside. This room doesn't even have a window.' I stood up and opened the door. Binesh said nothing.

We came back and sat down on the bed. There was a sheet spread unevenly on it. Under it was a quilt, most of which you could see.

'Do you have a gold ring?'

'Why?'

'I need it,' Binesh said.

'There's one in my suitcase, but it is broken.'

I unlocked the suitcase and took out, wrapped in a piece of newspaper, the two pieces of the ring. My elder sister had given it to me long ago. I liked wearing rings. I'd brought it from home and planned to wear it after getting it repaired.

As I was opening the packet one of the pieces fell on the bed. Binesh wanted to get up but I stopped him. I thought if he got up the piece might get lost. The bed sheet was crumpled. I smoothed it out and found the piece embedded in a crease. I asked Binesh to spread the bed sheet again. Binesh spread the bed sheet. Then we both sat down on it. The two pieces of the ring and the lump of metal lay on the newspaper between us.

'What will you do now?' I asked.

'I thought I'd compare the two and see.'

I too looked carefully at the piece Binesh had found, trying to decide. I thought the ring had a tinge of copper, unlike the metal piece which had a different brightness. 'The ring is not pure gold,' I said. 'It's mixed with something else. But yours looks hundred per cent gold.'

'So it does,' Binesh said.

'Where did you find it?' I asked, eager for an answer.

'On the street.'

'On the street!' I was surprised.

'Yes, I found it last evening. The minute I saw it I thought it was gold. I wanted to come and see you right away. I couldn't sleep properly. It would be marvellous if it is gold.'

'Why?' I asked.

'I don't have clothes. I'll sell it and get some stitched.'

'Must weigh five or six tolas,' I said. I picked up the piece and tried to guess its weight.

'What is the price of gold?'

'It is a hundred and twenty rupees per tola.'

'You'll get about five or six hundred rupees,' I said, making a quick calculation. 'What will you do with the rest of the money?'

'I'll buy some books, pay my tuition fee. I'll get a bed, a table and a chair. I'll give some money to my mother and put some in the post office.'

'Where will you sell it?'

'There's a goldsmith I know. I'd sold my mother's necklace to him once. The price of gold then was a hundred and thirty rupees per tola.'

'You decided to sell it on your own?'

'No, mother asked me to sell it.' He was getting irritated now.

'Suppose it turns out to be brass?'

'That's what I'm afraid of.' Binesh looked tired. I wrapped the two pieces of the ring in the newspaper and put it back in the trunk. Binesh kept holding the metal piece.

'Let's go to the goldsmith right away,' Binesh said.

'It's raining. We'll go in the evening.'

'It will stop raining just now,' he said.

The rain went on for a couple of hours. Binesh fell asleep. He was snoring, with one hand on the pocket of his shirt. I looked at him and hoped that the piece would turn out to be gold. The rain had stopped when he woke. There was a lot of bustle outside. He was angry with me for having let him sleep. I should have woken him. It must have stopped raining sometime back.

We made our way to the goldsmith. There was a lock on the door.

'Now what?' I asked.

'Let's go to another goldsmith.'

'If it turns out to be brass, won't he laugh at us?'

'No. No one will laugh.'

'I'm not going to ask him.'

'Okay, I will.'

There was a fifteen- or sixteen-year-old boy in front of the shop, cleaning silver jewellery in a basin full of soapy water. We walked past the shop a couple of times. The boy looked at us once, but we walked on as if we had nothing to say, at least to the boy. We returned without having made any enquiries.

I was hungry. It was my dinner time.

'I'm going to eat.'

'Where?'

'At the Marwari eatery,' I said. Binesh knew that I had my meals there.

'Come, eat at my place today.' He did not want to let go of me. He looked worried.

'What shall we do with this?'

'Listen,' I said. 'It must belong to some poor fellow. Let's give it back to him.'

'Who will you return it to?'

'The police station is near the eatery. We'll deposit it there.'

'No, let it be. I don't want to return it.'

'I think you should.'

'All right,' Binesh said resignedly. 'But you do the talking.'

'Yes, I'll do the talking.'

'Say that you found it. Don't mention me.'

'I won't,' I said.

He looked around and slipped me the piece of metal.

WE HAD COME AWAY from the police station feeling nervous. It was the first time we had been to one. We were sitting in the Marwari eatery. I'd been eating there for four months at twenty-five rupees a month. I'd asked Binesh if he wanted to join me but he refused.

'I think it was gold. The inspector must later have picked it up and kept it,' Binesh said. He looked sad. I too thought, as I ate, that it looked like gold, not like brass at all. The inspector thought we were fools. He said it was brass and quite worthless. Then, right in front of us, he chucked it outside.

'I too think it was gold. As soon as we turned our backs he must have gone and retrieved it,' I said.

We were quiet after that. Neither of us spoke. I was not liking the food and Binesh muttered something about my being a slow eater.

We came out after I'd finished eating. At first we walked slowly, then we started walking fast. When we came to the crossing, we turned towards the police station. Then we slowed down again. From a distance we saw the inspector busy with his papers. His khaki uniform looked smart on him, but as we came closer the uniform made us uncomfortable. We slipped past the inspector and came to the side of the road where he had thrown the piece and began to search for it. It was not long before we saw it lying next to the drain, the piece that had looked like gold. We looked at each other. Then we turned back. The piece was still lying there. When we came to the crossing and Binesh turned to go home, I asked him, 'Will you be coming to college tomorrow?'

'No.'

'Why?'

Binesh said nothing.

He was not looking at me. He was still wearing my unwashed clothes. He walked away.

1957–58

room on the tree

WHEN HE MOVED IN, he felt there were rats in the room. He only heard them at first, as they scurried along the rafters. Then he saw their faces, peeping out from between them. They looked like rats but had bushy tails. He realized they were squirrels and that rats and squirrels have similar features. Once he knew they were squirrels he felt more relaxed. His room, on the second floor, had only one window. The window had no shutters and overlooked the gutter at the back, where stood an old peepul tree. One of the tree's branches came right up to the window. Across from him he could see the backs of other houses, the same gutter running past them.

He'd been there a few days when it occurred to him that it might be possible to tame the squirrels. Lying in bed, he could see them come up to the table or to his tin trunk. When he first moved in, the distance between the bed and the table was only a handspan. Later, he pushed the bed right up against the table. He wanted to move around the room and work there. He wanted the squirrels to live with him; to enter the room without being scared; to sometimes try and get inside his pocket; to sit on his bed, close to the pillow; to climb onto his shoulder, etc. He hadn't seen more than three squirrels at a time in the room and had no idea how many lived in the peepul. If he knew someone had the answer he'd certainly have asked.

One day he entered the room and got a start. There was a pariah kite sitting on the window ledge. It flew out as soon as he opened the door. Had it been a crow, a parrot or any other attractive bird he wouldn't have been startled. In all his thirty years, he'd never seen a kite inside a room. He'd never imagined that such a thing could happen. He was afraid that the kite may have been after a squirrel. To reassure himself, he looked under the bed and in all the corners. Then he decided he'd meet the landlord and ask him to have shutters fitted in the window. He thought of the landlord as a kind man. He lay down on the bed.

From the bed he could see the green branch of the peepul. Nothing moved on it and he didn't see any birds, though he kept looking. A few times he even felt that he was living in a tree house. He'd been there for almost five months. Once, going up to his room in the evening, he felt as though he was climbing the peepul, though he didn't know how to climb trees. Maybe he was sad that day or had an upset stomach. He liked the idea of living in a secluded place, high above the ground, where his father, sisters or his friends wouldn't be able to reach him. No one had visited him in all the time he'd been there. He thought that his younger brother might come one day. His younger brother wanted to give up his studies and take up a job. He did not approve of this. When he locked the room to go to work, he felt as if he had bound the room hand and foot, not that there was any chance of the room climbing down after him. The room had not been easy to find. Had his brother rented a similar room on an upper floor, he would not want him to have the same thought while locking it.

Early next morning he went to see the landlord. He called out the landlord's name and almost immediately the door was opened by a thin man. Perhaps it was the servant who must have been standing there, right beside the door. The servant whispered, 'Speak softly. The landlord's asleep.'

Then the door was closed again. He could not tell whether the servant had gone away or was still there. He hadn't heard him walk away, so he must still be there. He paced about in front of the house. After a while the door opened again.

'Is it something important?' It was the servant.

'Yes it is,' he replied anxiously.

'Come in.'

He was led into a large room and hadn't even taken a proper look when the landlord appeared.

'What is it?'

'The window shutters. Can they be fitted tomorrow?'

'Any special reason?'

'No, nothing special. It's just that kites and crows get into the room, that's all.'

He hadn't mentioned the squirrels on purpose.

'You could nail two wooden slats crosswise to the window. You could also paint a man's face on a clay pot and hang it outside. It will scare off the birds, even when you're not in the room. Are you afraid of them?'

The landlord was smiling. Or maybe he wasn't.

'No, I'm not. But the peepul branch that's right outside the room bothers me. A chameleon got in a couple of days ago. It had a red face and only ran away when I picked up a book. Two of my fingers brushed against it. I believe they're poisonous.'

It was a lie. No one had told him that chameleons were poisonous.

'Which two fingers? Can you show me,' said the landlord. He was taking this seriously.

'These two.' He opened the index and middle fingers of his right hand, keeping the others closed.

'Okay, I'll have the shutters put in tomorrow. Just be careful for today.'

They both stood there quietly. The landlord was looking for something. The shutters would keep out squirrels too, he thought to himself. He wanted to keep out the crows and kites, but not squirrels. Mightn't it be better to have iron bars put instead? They'd serve the purpose.

'No, let's not have shutters. We can put iron bars in the window.'

The landlord looked at him and thought that he looked a little sad.

'Iron bars?'

'Bars will keep out the kites and crows. It's a nuisance to keep opening and shutting the window.'

'I have some planks lying around. They can be used for the shutters. The bars can be put in later.'

'Can't you get the bars put in first? The shutters can wait.' He was almost pleading.

'What are you going on about?' said the landlord, irritably. 'You say you are afraid of chameleons, but even snakes can slip in through the bars. You think there are no snakes on trees?'

He returned to his room. He tried to see if the windows he passed had iron bars. There were a couple of shisham trees by the side of the road; in fact there were quite a few. He saw a crow sitting on one of them. There was a constant traffic of cars. He couldn't have seen many windows and shisham trees because of it.

He'd hoped to see a squirrel and found one sitting near his shoe. Though he'd opened the door softly, he still managed to scare it. He took off his chappals near the door and went in. The squirrel gave a few jerky movements of the head and was out of the window and onto the tree. He rushed to the window but couldn't see it. He kept looking at the tree, trying to figure out whether a snake could get into the room from there. He couldn't tell. It was evening. He stretched out his hand and plucked a green leaf. He tore the leaf lengthwise into two halves and rolled one of them into a hollow pipe. He blew into it but nothing happened; it made no sound. His younger brother was clever at these things. He felt like whispering his younger brother's name to hear how it sounded. He moved away from the window and went to the door to put on his chappals. He whispered 'Saddhan, Saddhan, Saddhan' three times and listened to his own voice. He then bolted the door.

He lay down on the charpoy. It was a little dark. He put on the light. He could see the peepul branch and its leaves. Once in a while the leaves stirred. There were crows cawing in the tree. Their sound seemed to come from an adjoining room, but there was no other room. There was only his room at one end of the branch. All of a sudden the electric bulb started to become dim and the room began to lose light. He felt as though the room had had a puncture and the light escaping from it was like air escaping from a tube. He got up. He went up to the roof and vomited.

He heard a knock; it made him open the door and come out. It was the landlord's servant. There was an ancient-looking carpenter with him. He was carrying two planks of wood on his left shoulder and a dirty bag made of burlap in his right hand. His tools must have been in the bag.

'Are the window shutters to be put in?' asked the carpenter.

'The landlord has sent us,' the servant said.

'But I'm about to leave for office.'

'It won't take long, just a couple of hours.' The servant looked at the carpenter who was sitting on the ground and taking out his tools one by one.

'Are the iron bars not going to be fixed then?'

'The landlord didn't say anything about them.'

'I don't want to have shutters.'

'Well, it's up to you.' The servant sounded irritable. The old carpenter had stopped taking out the tools. There must have been only a couple left in the bag.

'Wait. I'll go and speak with the landlord,' he said. The servant was grumbling. The carpenter also looked annoyed. He dressed quickly and came out. He had combed his hair. He locked the room. The carpenter had put all the tools back into the bag.

'We'll wait here,' said the servant. He was now sitting on one of the planks.

'No, you come with me.'

He was afraid they might force open the lock and put in the shutters even though he'd told them not to.

He followed the carpenter who was slowly going down the stairs. The servant was behind him. The planks were left where they were.

'Wait!' he said. The three of them stopped on the stairs.

'We've left the planks on the roof,' he said anxiously, looking at the servant.

'We'll take them later. They might still be needed.'

'Someone could steal them,' he said, going up one step. The servant didn't move.

'No one will steal the planks,' said the servant.

They came down after that. The landlord wasn't around. He didn't go to office that day. He vacated the room and moved into a dharmshala. He did not have a lot of stuff. The charpoy and the table belonged to the landlord.

HE WAS LIVING IN a set of two rooms he'd rented cheaply in one of the inner lanes of the city. For a few days he felt unsettled in the new place. The scuttling of rats reminded him of the squirrels. He kept dreaming about a zoo. After a while he went to see his old room. Going up the familiar stairs he became emotional and began to miss home. He did not feel that he was climbing a peepul tree. The door was closed. An old man opened it when he knocked. He looked as old as his father. For a moment he thought it was his father.

'Yes?' said the old man.

'Excuse me, I used to live in this room,' he said, glancing inside.

'Oh! Do come in. Why did you leave ? You must have found a better place.' The old man moved aside to let him come in. They were now both inside the room. He noticed the bars and shutters in the window. It was open.

'Do you always leave the window open?'

'Yes, I do. It gets quite humid during the rains.'

'There must be squirrels coming in from the peepul.' They were both looking at the window.

'I've been here twelve days but haven't seen a squirrel. There are rats, though,' said the old man, looking up at the rafters.

'At first that's what I thought too,' he said, pleased. 'You think they're rats, but they're really squirrels. Once they get used to you you'll be able to see them. I'm surprised they haven't so far. When I lived here they'd sit on the table and I'd observe them from the bed. Initially they were shy. I kept the table pushed up against the window and my cot against the table.' He said all this in one breath.

'Where did you hang your clothes?' asked the old man.

'On that nail, where you've hung your shirt. I was the one who put them in. Who put the nails on the other wall, I don't know.'

'Then why did you leave the room?'

'The window didn't have bars or shutters when I was here. Crows and kites would come into the room. Tell me, can't a snake also come in from the peepul?'

'No, I don't think so.'

'But snakes do live in trees.'

'Yes, that's what they say.'

'So you have no problems with this place?'

'Well, it's a little hard going up and down the stairs. Nothing else.'

He noticed that the gutter looked like a small river because it was filled with rainwater. There was no smell either. He liked the room even more than before.

'How long will you be here for?'

'A couple of months. I have a little work to do. Then I'll move to the city.'

'I think I'll come back to this room once you leave.'

'Yes, I was lucky to find it. It's a nice room.'

'Has anyone come asking for me?'

'Not since I've been here.'

Without giving the old man a chance to ask anything further, he said namaste and left. He felt sad that he'd given up the room. He went straight to the landlord, without worrying what the landlord might think of his old tenant who had left so abruptly. The landlord had not forgotten him. In fact, he looked happy to see him.

'I'd like to come back to the room. I'm sad that I left it. Please let me know when it falls vacant again.'

'I had bars and shutters put in the window only because you wanted them.'

'Yes, I know. Will you charge the same rent?'

'Yes, of course. I haven't raised it.'

As he entered the lane to go home, he realized that he hadn't told the landlord where he lived. He turned to go back and spotted the servant coming towards him. He suspected he was being followed. This made him uneasy and instead of going home he started to walk in a different direction.

He never returned to the room on the peepul tree. Perhaps he was afraid of the snake that lived there. He had no wish to die. He could imagine, were he to die, the straits his family would be in. And it wasn't as if he could keep the window shut at all times. He still hoped to be able to tame squirrels.

1965

spare time of the crowd

'STOP! DON'T ANYONE LEAVE,' he said, addressing the passers-by. The road had been newly repaired and there was an empty drum of coal tar by its side. It had been upended. Beside it, on the ground, was a red warning flag. Traffic had resumed but there were few vehicles. When people saw a neatly turned out man standing on the drum and shouting, they stopped to listen. Soon there was a crowd. A man wearing a shirt and trousers, with a tilak on his forehead, was coming from the opposite direction. He paused briefly, then resumed walking. He seemed to be a pandit.

'Hey you!' the man who was standing on the drum shouted angrily. The crowd turned and looked towards the pandit. The pandit did not stop. When he noticed this, the man on the drum said to the crowd, 'Brothers! That man's paying no attention to me. Stop him from leaving.' People started pushing each other to get to the pandit. Seeing the crowd, the pandit, who had no idea why it was coming towards him, started running. He was finally caught by some boys who brought him back, holding him firmly by the arm as if he might try to escape again. They dragged him to the front and gathered round the man who was standing on the drum. A middle-aged woman had appeared and squeezed herself in quietly at the back of the crowd. She was wearing glasses and carried a sling-bag. She was probably the headmistress of a primary school. No one had noticed her coming. They were all looking at the man on the upturned drum and at the pandit. The man on the drum was wearing a freshly washed shirt, with sleeves rolled up to the elbows. When he raised his right hand, the two gold rings on his fingers glinted in the sun.

'My shoes pinch but I can't walk without shoes,' he said, his rings glittering.

'So what can we do about it?' the pundit said irritably, trying to free his arm from the boys. They tightened their grip.

'Why don't you let me go?' The pundit was now almost pleading.

'Not before you've heard what he has to say,' said the boy who was holding his right arm. He was wearing a kurta and pajama and had large eyes. He looked well-to-do and had a serious expression.

'I said that my shoes pinch but I cannot go barefoot,' the man who was standing on the drum shouted again.

'Is there anything we can do to help?' someone asked from the crowd, sounding sympathetic.

'There are blisters on my feet and I have a long way to go. Now you tell me what I should do.'

'You poor man! Your shoes must be new. Walk around a little, by and by they'll become soft and won't pinch.'

When they heard a woman's loud voice at the back, people turned round to see who it was. It was the middle-aged woman with the sling-bag. At once, almost respectfully, they made way for her. She arranged the folds of her white sari that had a broad border and, no part of her touching any of the men standing there, came up to the front.

'It's not that my shoes are new. I don't know what's wrong with them. They didn't pinch earlier,' the man on the drum said.

'Let me go,' the pandit said peevishly. Nobody paid any attention to him.

'Did you walk on this road that's just been repaired?' said a thin, sickly-looking man.

'I did walk on it for about half a furlong but then I came back. My feet really hurt when I was walking.'

'There you are. That's what it is then,' said the sickly-looking man. 'Your shoes may be old, but the road is new. Maybe that's why they pinch.'

'Possibly,' said the man who was standing on the drum, sounding helpless.

'My shoes are old too, but how come they don't pinch?' asked an elderly man.

'That's because you haven't walked on this stretch of road before. You were a few steps ahead of me and I noticed you because of the way you have of swinging your right arm. It must be a habit. The newly repaired stretch begins from the spot where we're standing now.' The middle-aged woman was clever.

Then someone else said, 'I've also come by this road and had no trouble at all.' The crowd fell silent.

'But you're wearing chappals. Maybe it's only shoes that pinch and not chappals,' said his friend who was standing next to the man in chappals. Some people looked at his feet.

'I've never heard of chappals pinching,' said another man.

'Let's put it to the test. We'll get a person who is wearing shoes to walk on the road and then we'll see if the shoes pinch,' said one of the boys.

Someone looked at the pandit's feet and cried out, 'He's wearing shoes.'

'I'm not going to walk,' said the pandit. At some point the boys had let go of his arm but now they caught hold of it again. There were half a dozen people who were wearing shoes, but none was willing to walk on the road.

'How will I go now?' the man on the drum asked sadly. 'I have a long way to walk. The road goes on for about four miles.'

'Can't you turn back and go by another road?' the middle-aged woman said, her eyes filling with tears. She took off her glasses.

'What are you talking about? There is no other road,' the serious-looking boy snapped at her.

'It's not that I know all the roads in this town,' she said. 'I've only come here recently on transfer and am learning my way around. I still haven't found a cheap place to stay. I don't know what to do.'

'Nothing is easy here,' someone said. To which someone else added, 'Don't you have a son? How long are you going to manage on your own?'

'No, I don't have a son. I have a daughter and she's married. Her husband gives her a hard time.'

'And what about your husband?' the pandit asked the middle-aged woman.

'He died four years ago.' The middle-aged woman, who was already sad because the serious-looking boy had scolded her, now burst into tears. When they saw her crying, people in the crowd began to whisper to each other: 'Do you know of a place that she might rent?' 'The poor woman's husband died. She'll find it difficult in her old age.' 'She should have had a couple of sons. Then it might not have been so bad.' 'Well, I know of a house that's going, but it won't suit her.'

She was still crying. No one was paying much attention to the man who was standing on the drum. He finally lost his temper and yelled, 'Brothers! I have another four miles to go. I don't want to hire a rickshaw or a tonga. And my shoes pinch.'

The crowd was quiet again. 'Well, don't go on talking about yourself,' said the pandit.

'What should I do then,' the man who was standing on the drum said. He seemed to have no ideas of his own.

'Let's first listen to what he has to say,' the middle-aged woman said. She'd stopped crying.

'Well, you could take off your shoes and walk barefoot,' someone suggested.

'How will he walk for four miles without shoes? Didn't he say he had blisters on his feet?' said another man.

'Do you really have blisters on your feet?' asked the pandit disbelievingly. 'Show me.'

The man standing on the drum swayed a little as he tried to take off his shoes, but then spread his arms in the air and managed to keep his balance. He'd groaned while taking off the shoes. His blisters must have hurt. The shoes were tight.

They saw that he had large blisters on both feet, near the big toe.

'Ooh!' said the crowd when it saw the blisters. The middle-aged woman was the first to exclaim.

'Where did you buy the shoes from?' asked one of the boys angrily.

'The best one is Ramchandani's,' said an elderly man.

'No, Laljirao's is the best. You can get good shoes there at a reasonable price. I've been wearing these shoes for the last four years and they're as good as new,' said one of the men, bringing his right foot to his left knee so that people could get a good look at the sole. It did look new.

'We have to give it to you,' someone said appreciatively, as people came closer to get a better look.

'Show me. I didn't see,' said another, with a curiosity that was only to be expected. The man raised his foot again for the shoe to be scrutinized. The middle-aged woman also wanted to take a look, but she wasn't able to.

'Surely he's lying. It cannot be that the sole has worn down in four years only as little as it would have in two days,' said the pandit.

'He must be working for Lalji,' the middle-aged woman said with a knowledgeable air.

'I think the man on the drum also works for Lalji,' said the elderly man.

'But how did he get blisters on his feet?' asked the middle-aged woman.

'He must have burnt them on purpose, or used a chemical to blister his feet,' said the pandit. This gave the crowd something to talk about.

'Anything can happen nowadays.'

'They smear their skin with paint and oil to make it look like they've got leprosy. People feel sorry for them and give them money. You'd be convinced they were lepers if you saw them.'

'Why, they even stick live maggots in their wounds.'

'Where do they get them from?'

'It's not as if there's a shortage of maggots. You can find them easily.'

'These people are filthy. They breed them in their homes.'

The man who was standing on the drum was red with anger. He'd put on his shoes and had his hands in his pockets. Someone noticed this and asked, 'You got maggots in them?'

'Lots,' said the man on the drum. 'And I'm about to throw them on you.' A flutter went through the crowd.

'No, please don't do that. I've been listening to you very carefully and I do feel for you,' said the middle-aged woman. She was worried about what he'd just said.

'Whatever,' said the man. 'Here!' And taking out his tightly closed fists from his pockets, made as if to fling something at the crowd. He had thrown nothing, but people began to push and jostle as though he had, trying to get out of the way. It was only an act he was putting on to show how angry he was. In a frenzy, he again flung the imaginary maggots from his empty fists towards the crowd. In the meantime, the pandit was running hard on the newly repaired road, but no one noticed him.

The man got down from the drum and melted into the crowd. Later, people found out that he'd only been pretending about the maggots. It was just that he was distressed at his own plight. The crowd came back. Because of all the commotion, there were more people now than before. A car had got stuck in the crowd. When they heard the horn, people made way for it. The car turned and seemed to glide along on the road that had just been repaired. Everyone stood there and watched it disappear.

Then for no apparent reason they went and knocked down the drum on which the man had been standing. They rolled it to the middle of the road and stood it upright. The serious-looking boy picked up the pole with the red warning flag on it and put it inside the drum, with the flag sticking out.

'The road is closed for repairs,' said the elderly man. The crowd slowly dispersed. The man whose shoe had been pinching limped off in the opposite direction. The middle-aged woman went and stood on the veranda of a closed shop, breathing heavily as she looked at the thinning crowd. The elderly man went past her but she did not notice if he moved his right arm awkwardly when he walked. The shops were yet to open and there weren't many people around.

1965

the man's woman

I WALKED UP TO the garden with Jainath as if I was not walking with Jainath.

As soon as we came to the lawn, he lay down, flat on his back, without worrying about dirtying his white clothes. I did not want to sit but I did. The grass had not been cut for a long time. The garden was like the ruin of a garden.

'Let's go home,' I said.

'Whose home?'

'You go to yours and I'll go to mine,' I said.

'Let's both go to your home,' Jainath said. He said this as though, besides us, there was a third person present, and that third person was also me.

Jainath had stretched out his arms on the lawn and clutched the grass in his fists as though he was mercilessly pulling his son's hair. But he did not have a son. He was staring at the sky without blinking. Seeing him, I too looked up. There was a pariah kite wheeling in the sky. Looking at Jainath lying on the grass, I wondered if the kite might think he was a corpse. I stood up and started pacing about. I did this because I did not want the kite to have a similar thought about me.

'Did you speak with the doctor?' Jainath asked. He still had the grass clenched in his fists. If the grass had been a little longer, it would have looked as if he'd seized his wife's hair. He had a wife. Her name was Krishnabai.

The name was tattooed on her right arm. Jainath wanted to have it erased. His wife was fair, which made the greenish colour of the letters stand out all the more. They could be read easily. I'd never seen his wife. When I saw a thorny green vine wrapped around a nearby utility pole, I decided that this was a Krishnabai growing on the pole. I also thought that I should pluck a leaf from it and crush it in my hand. I plucked a green leaf and squeezed a green drop from it on my palm. 'What are you doing?' asked Jainath.

'Let's go home. We'll think of something. I'm worried about you,' I said, rubbing my palms together.

I saw that when Jainath loosened his grip, the flattened grass began to straighten up slowly. I took a deep breath; it was as though the trampled grass had done so too. I immediately felt less tense.

'I'll cut off her arm,' Jainath said, rising to his feet.

'That's okay, to chop off her arm, but will you sever it from the elbow or from the shoulder?' I asked quickly, after hesitating. He had started to walk towards the road as though he hadn't heard me.

'Wait,' I said, looking at his back. There were a few green stains from the crushed grass on Jainath's white shirt and trousers. Had the grass been red I'd have thought of bloodstains. I was happy now.

'What is it?' asked Jainath.

'Why do you need to chop off her arm? There's something else you can do. You can erase the tattoo with a razor blade.' I felt Jainath hadn't paid attention to what I'd said. We came to a road that we had to cross. A bus coming from the right sped past, then a tonga went by. We crossed the road when there was no traffic except for two pedestrians coming from the left.

After walking some distance I asked Jainath, 'Which way should we go?' 'This way,' he said, turning to the right and still walking with his head bent and his eyes on the ground. A little ahead of us, at the edge of a field, were three ugly-looking houses. There was a pig rooting about. I pointed in their direction and said to Jainath, 'See, that's your wife's name engraved right there. Three ugly-looking houses and a pig. It's so very "Krishnabai". The pig is the "i" of Krishnabai.' Jainath turned left. I walked beside him. This was the road that led to my house.

IT WAS AROUND SEVEN in the evening. Jainath came to my house wearing clean trousers and a white shirt. He sat down on the charpoy. As soon as he sat down, I noticed he clenched the bed sheet in his fists and the crinkles, where he had clenched the sheet, spread out from his fists to the rest of the bed. 'This is a really bad habit of yours,' I said to him irritably, smoothing down the bed sheet. Jainath looked grave. I'd put on the light in the room. I was sitting on an old chair in front of the charpoy.

First Jainath talked of this and that. Outside, the children of the neighbourhood were creating a ruckus. Then, without missing a detail, he told me how yesterday he'd tried to remove the name from his wife's arm with a new razor blade. His wife had been scrubbing utensils. He first checked his shaving kit, but it didn't have a new blade. He asked his wife for some money and went out to buy one. The thought did come to him that he could try to do the job with the old blade that he'd used only once. (At this point I said, 'And then?') He had the new blade with him. His wife had finished cleaning the utensils. He called out to her. He caught hold of her right hand, it was still wet, and told her that he was going to remove the tattoo. There'd be no pain. His wife was frightened. She ran to a corner of the courtyard and stood there. She did not say anything. He was angry at first, then he cajoled her. He went out to the courtyard and, grabbing her hand, brought her back to the room. (I again said, 'Then?' Jainath was looking good to me today.) He made his wife sit down in a corner of the room. He sat down too, but realized that it would be easier if he stood up to do the job. He had to be very careful. He made his wife also stand up and lean against the wall. He pressed against her with his shoulder and tried to scrape off the name with the razor blade. It was a new blade so there were a lot of small cuts. He was only able to get to the 'Kri' of 'Krishnabai'. His clothes were stained with blood. 'Were these the clothes you were wearing?' I asked, looking at his washed shirt.

'Yes,' said Jainath.

'You must have washed them yesterday?'

'Yes. There is a wound on my wife's arm,' Jainath said. I stood up and began to pace the room. Then I sat down again. My brain was not working. I wanted my brain to work. So I reached out and picked up a scrap of paper from the window ledge. I tore it into shreds and threw the shredded paper out of the window. I noticed that the neighbourhood boys were silent. All this I did sitting on the chair.

'The wound has almost healed. Some penicillin ointment was lying in the house. She refused to apply it at first.'

'Tell me something,' I said. 'Did you apply the ointment only on "Kri" or did you spread it over all the letters?'

Jainath said, 'The wound was only on "Kri", but I don't remember. Maybe the ointment spread till "Krishna". I am very worried. The whole mohalla knows her name. It's written in big letters, from below the elbow to the wrist. The tattoo is visible from a distance.'

His eyes had filled with tears. I felt sorry for him. I got up and made some tea while he sat there looking sad. Then he lay down on the bed. Had there been a calendar in front of him on the wall, with the picture of a woman or a child, he'd have looked at it lovingly. It was already quite late. 'Go home,' I said. 'Your wife must be waiting.'

It was past eleven. He looked lost. He didn't want to leave. Then both of us planned how next time round he should use sulphuric acid. It didn't look any different from water. If he tried, he could buy the acid quite easily. He'd make his wife sit down on the pretext of applying ointment to her wound. He'd act affectionately towards her and then pour the whole bottle on her arm. The acid would come out with a gurgling sound. If she screamed, he'd let her; he wouldn't be scared by it. To stop her from screaming too loudly, he'd put his hand over her mouth. He'd make sure that no acid fell on him.

'Okay,' said Jainath. He looked happy when he left my house at around two. I slept well that night and got up late the next morning. My limbs were aching.

I HADN'T SEEN JAINATH for many days. I thought he hadn't been able to do the job. Maybe he hadn't been able to get the sulphuric acid. Maybe his wife had resisted and some of the acid had fallen on him. The chances though of this happening were slim, because Jainath was strong. He wasn't tall but he was well built. I knew that his wife was thin, almost sickly. Nonetheless, I was worried about Jainath. I wondered what he was up to.

For the next few days I spent my spare time in places where I was likely to run into him. I thought I had lost weight.

One morning Jainath woke me early. 'Come!' he said. I was glad to see him. I got up and started to get ready, preparing to have a leisurely chat with him. But he seemed to be in some hurry and this made me lose my temper.

'Did you do the job?' was the first thing I asked him, angrily.

'No,' he said, becoming sad.

'Then I won't go,' I said, and taking off the trousers I'd just put on, I hung them up on a peg. Then I lay down on the bed. It took much persuasion from him before I agreed to go.

He was taking me to his place. I caught a glimpse of a woman on the roof of his house from afar. Then she must have sat down suddenly because she'd seen us coming. It must be Jainath's wife, I thought. Jainath hadn't seen her. He almost ran up the stairs and by the time I reached the top he'd got his wife to open the door. He was standing at the door, alone. His wife wasn't there.

'Why didn't you do it?' I whispered when we were in the room.

'I couldn't find any acid.'

'You should have told me earlier.'

'I didn't get the chance to tell you.'

'I'll bring the acid tomorrow.'

'Okay, we can try doing it with acid. Will it be fixed then, once and for all?' Jainath asked. Then he pointed to the bed. 'What is it?' I said to him. We'd both come up to the bed. I saw 'Krishnabai' embroidered in uneven letters on the new pillow cover. This came as a surprise. 'I love her,' said Jainath softly. I swore at him in my head. I was listening to what Jainath said, and in my head I was listening also to the profanities I had used for him.

Jainath said that he'd asked his wife if she did embroidery. She'd said yes, but had hesitated. Then he brought home a new pillow cover, a needle, and threads of many colours. He asked his wife to embroider leaves and flowers on the pillow and, after some thought, to embroider her name as well. She suspected something was wrong and at first had refused. It was only when he lost his temper and hit her on the back with his fist that she agreed.

'Let me see,' I said to Jainath. He picked up the pillow and showed it to me. I looked at it carefully and saw that she had indeed embroidered her name. There was no mistaking it. I came away. Jainath was a beast, I thought, and stopped being friends with him. I never brought any acid to give Jainath.

1965

the gathering

ALL OF A SUDDEN a man appeared. He looked tired and carried a heavy sack over his shoulder. He was covered in sweat. His clothes were filthy and he had a stubble. He hadn't combed his hair. 'Hey, hey,' everyone shouted joyfully when they saw him. They helped him lower the sack and place it in the centre of the gathering. He sat down and rested his back against it. His gaze was lowered and he was breathing hard. He'd been missing for fifteen days.

They were all poets. The man who had just come too was a poet. They were young and bright-eyed. A middle-aged man was also there. He was a critic.

'Have we got all the symbols we need?' the critic asked contemptuously.

'No, I couldn't find the one-petalled rose,' said the man who'd come with the sack.

'Why?'

'I couldn't find one, that's all.' He sounded irritable.

'Tell me, why do you write such long poems? Surely a man's life is more than some useless things. You brought a bald truck tyre once.'

'Well, I did explain what it symbolized.'

'You couldn't even have made a pair of chappals out of it. I'll have the tyre thrown out of the godown tomorrow. A poem isn't a rubbish dump where you can chuck what you like –

cigarette stubs, cracked mirrors, broken crockery – and always with the excuse that they're symbols. You must have brought the same rotten things again. Is there nothing you can bring that is undamaged? And does a one-petalled rose even exist? But let's presume that you find one. It still doesn't do anything for the poem. The rose will wilt in an hour or two. You'll have to get rid of that line about the rose,' said the critic angrily.

'Well, I'm not going to.' He was still breathless. 'Where will I find the one-petalled rose? Over the last fifteen days I've visited many gardens, looking for it. But there's a way out.' He took a red rose from a vase that stood in a corner. Everyone looked solemnly at what he was doing.

'I'll tear off all the petals except one. Then it will be a one-petalled rose. It's not as if roses never wilt or don't have their petals torn off.'

He'd got this idea from the labourer-poet who hadn't been able to make it to the gathering for the last two years. His poems were always about rotis. He'd set out after a day of hard work to come to the gathering, carrying the rotis with him. But at some point he'd get hungry and eat the rotis. He'd met him a short while ago, when the labourer-poet, after having come halfway, was about to turn back. By going on and on about the common man, the labourer-poet had said, the critic was misleading everyone.

'This is being dishonest to the poem as well as to the reader,' shouted the critic. 'I'm not going to put up with it. You're expelled from the group forthwith. This is the last time you're going to read here. The godown is already overflowing with your rotten symbols.'

'That's fine by me. I don't need your godown any more. You are a literary bureaucrat who arm-twists people into doing your bidding. I love my symbols. They're not saleable commodities. You want me to put hundred-rupee notes as symbols in my poems so you can deposit them in the godown. So what if I have to steal to get the money, while you just sit here doing nothing. The truth is that I've never even seen a hundred-rupee note. As for my inability to see anything whole, you're absolutely right. My life is entirely about broken things.'

'True. True,' the poets said, agreeing with him.

The critic didn't seem upset in the least. 'Friends,' he began, 'there's nothing to be agitated about. We'd agreed that before they start reading, each poet will show us the symbols they've used in the poem. The reason for this is that no one should afterwards say that poets are cut off from reality. Things that exist in the real world exist also in our poems. What makes symbols new is not simply that we haven't come across them in our daily lives. Newness lies in how symbols are used. Friends, there's another thing. The experiment we're conducting has not been done before; it's an experiment in poetry as well as an experiment in reading. For the first time the audience will be able to physically see the symbols in the poem even as the poem is being read. It will be the poem revealed. While it is true that the revealed poem is only a part of our own ordinary lives being revealed, we seldom give the revelation a second thought. We may have climbed the same staircase for decades, but if someone were suddenly to ask us the number of steps in it we'd be stuck for an answer. We mustn't forget that in today's world the poet is a failure.'

'You're right, absolutely right,' the poets said, agreeing with the critic.

The symbols mentioned in the poems were taken out of the sack and displayed. There was a dead snake that had ants sticking to its mouth, a dented aluminium cooking pot, a blue envelope that was as good as new, and other such things. The arrangement of symbols in the display followed the order in which they would appear in the poems. The poet then read from his work. The line about the rose with one petal had been removed. Some people applauded, others remained silent. Then they all looked at the critic.

The critic did not say anything immediately. After a while he said, 'There's no mention in your poem of a dead snake with ants sticking to its mouth.'

'No, there isn't.'

'But the dead snake you've brought has ants sticking to its mouth.'

Everyone present was astonished to hear this, for no one had noticed the absence of the ants in the poem.

'You must change either the poem or the symbol you've brought,' the critic advised.

The poet washed the snake's head and got rid of the ants. He then returned everything to the sack.

It was the turn of the Marwari poet next. The critic liked him. He wrote short poems and didn't need to bring a bag stuffed with symbols. His coat and trouser pockets were quite enough. He drank water from a silver tumbler and there was a tumbler in his poem. He produced the tumbler, two yards of gold thread and some shorter pieces of similar thread from his pocket. Then he read out the poem. It was a short love poem. The critic measured the gold thread to confirm that it was indeed two yards long, as the poem said it was. Next to the critic's room was a godown where the poets were supposed to keep the items they had used as symbols. Some of these things were expensive. This was why the critic always kept the godown locked. The poet who'd come with the sack added the items from it to the hundreds of others already there. They belonged to different poems and were arranged accordingly. He was surrounded with countless strange-looking symbols and felt as if his poems had been taken advantage of. In fact, he felt this about everyone's poems.

There was a ghostly atmosphere in the godown. He saw a petrol can. It was one of the symbols. Another symbol was a matchbox. His eyes lit up. He sprinkled petrol everywhere and set a match to it. Soon there was a blazing fire. He ran as fast as he could, out of the back door. He was afraid he'd get burnt. There was a stampede. The critic came running. He remembered the symbol kept next to the door: a fire extinguisher. He used it to douse the flames. There wasn't much damage. To the crowd that had gathered and to the few remaining poets, the critic proudly explained the usefulness of symbols.

1964

shoe ashtray

BAIKUNTH GOT UP. I kept sitting and pretended that I was reading the newspaper. He slipped his feet into his chappals and went to the bookshelf. He took out a book, flipped through it, but did not return it to the shelf. I thought he would now look at me but he did not. I was still pretending to read the newspaper when I saw him go towards the big table. He opened a drawer and took out a bunch of keys. They were long keys and shone like silver. I wondered why I had been observing Baikunth so keenly. Somehow it did not seem right. There were also two identical-looking small tables in the room. On one of them was a shoe ashtray, kept there as a piece of decoration. It was pretty.

Baikunth was still rummaging through the drawer. He was holding the bunch of keys in his left hand. Recently I'd come upon a bunch of rusty keys while cleaning my house. There were sixteen of them, all different, strung together on a metal wire. This is something that I must tell Baikunth about, I thought to myself. We'd been sitting there for a while without speaking a word.

'Why do you keep the keys in a drawer? And it isn't even locked,' I said. As soon as I said this I thought I'd said the wrong thing. Baikunth turned towards me but was still not looking at me. I decided if he looked at me now I wouldn't return his look. I found it hard to look at him and talk with him at the same time.

Baikunth held the keys tightly in his right fist. They were long keys and stuck out of his fist. He must have been surprised that I paid so much attention to what he did. Since he hadn't answered my question, I thought it was unlikely that he'd do so now. I felt awful. What Baikunth did should have been no concern of mine. I just had to wait patiently for Kakka to return. In order not to look at Baikunth, I turned my attention to the shoe ashtray and once again noticed how pretty it was.

'It's because of the servants,' Baikunth said at last. 'I never keep them in the same place. I keep shifting them around. If you lock away the keys, you'll still have a key to worry about. It's probably better this way.'

Perhaps he wanted to go to the other room.

'So long as you don't put them in a place where the servants can come upon them by accident,' I said, getting up.

'I'm here all the time. Haven't seen anyone stealing,' Baikunth said.

We'd come into the other room as we talked. I found I still had the newspaper in my hand. It felt like a burden. I wanted to put it down somewhere.

There were two newish steel almirahs in the room, and in a corner an old iron strongbox. A dust-covered raincoat was hanging on a peg. I was standing near the raincoat. The room was small.

'Did Kakka buy these almirahs recently?' I asked.

'He bought them a couple of months after we moved to this house.'

'Must have paid around two hundred and fifty for each?'

'No, five hundred.'

Baikunth stood in front of one of the almirahs, blocking my view. I moved to the left. I was a little curious to see what was inside.

He was trying to pick out a key from the bunch that he had in his hand. They all looked the same, except one which looked old. It must have been the key to the strongbox. As Baikunth unlocked the almirah, the right-hand door swung open. The other one remained closed. I could see what was inside but not very clearly; there were two or three bundles of currency notes kept on the side that was closed. Maybe that's why Baikunth did not want to open it in front of me.

'Look how much dust there is on the raincoat,' I said, wiping the dust with my finger.

I heard the almirah door being banged shut, and turned around. The first thing I saw was Baikunth hugging with his right hand several bundles of one-rupee notes to his chest. There were seven bundles in all.

'Kakka had asked for five hundred,' I said.

'The petrol bill has to be paid. You lock the almirah,' Baikunth said, handing me the key. 'Check the handle and see that it's locked properly.'

I pressed down the handle and found that it was not locked. I tried to lock it again but couldn't. I wondered why it wouldn't lock.

'Here, hold the money. Let me try.'

I hesitated, then took the money from him. I was holding the bundles carefully, perhaps too carefully.

We came back to the room where we'd been sitting. I wondered why Baikunth did not open the other door of the cupboard. I put down the money on the table. Baikunth called the servant and asked, 'Did he tell you to bring five hundred?'

The servant nodded. Baikunth handed over the money and said, 'Tell Kakka this is five hundred.'

Baikunth was Kakka's younger son. Ever since we were children, we'd called our uncle Kakka, which is why Baikunth too had also started calling him that. I saw him stuffing the remaining two bundles of notes in his trouser pockets. The pockets bulged. He was sitting on the chair, playing with the keys.

'Five hundred's a lot of money. What if the servant runs away with it?' I asked Baikunth.

'We ought to trust them a little,' Baikunth said. 'After all, where will he go?'

Five hundred rupees worth of trust was a lot of trust. I could have taken the money to Kakka, I thought to myself. It would have given me an excuse to meet him.

'I'm thirsty. But I prefer to have water from the surahi.' I really was very thirsty.

'The surahi is in the kitchen,' Baikunth said. I could have taken water from the fridge, but the glass water bottles clinked when you closed it, and I was afraid that something might break.

When I returned from the kitchen I found Baikunth still in the chair, but immediately noticed that he did not have the keys with him. He must have kept them somewhere. I sat down. I'd been waiting for Kakka for almost two hours and was bored.

'Looks like Kakka won't be home before evening,' I said.

'It's almost time for lunch. He should be here in half an hour,' Baikunth said with a yawn. He too looked bored. He must have had things to do and was only here because of me. We didn't have much to say to each other.

'I'll be off now. I'll see Kakka in the evening.'

'Is there anything in particular that you wanted to tell him?' Baikunth said. 'I could convey it for you.'

I did not really want to tell Baikunth. The BSc results had come out six days ago and I was hoping that Kakka would help me find a job. I said nothing to Baikunth.

'I think someone's at the door. I'll be back soon,' Baikunth said, scratching the floor with his bare toes to find his chappals.

I was alone in the room. I sat there for a while doing nothing. Then I went to the bookshelf. I put back the book that Baikunth had left lying outside. At that point I remembered the keys. I was curious to see if Baikunth had put them in the drawer. It would be some time before he returned. I went and quickly checked. The keys were not there. A small cockroach came out of the drawer and climbed onto my hand. It fell when I jerked my hand and disappeared under the bookshelf. The house felt empty. I sat down on the chair. Baikunth was not back. I did not want to think that he might have hidden the keys because I was in the house. Maybe he had them in his pocket. I looked out of the door and figured that he wouldn't be coming back soon. I ran my hand behind the books on the shelf, but the keys weren't there either, nor were they in the alcove. There was a large tin box on the table; it was full of tobacco. I tried to think of the other places where Baikunth might have hidden them. He must have put them in his pocket. It does happen sometimes that you put things in your pocket without thinking. It may have had nothing to do with me. Now that I had a reasonable idea of where the keys might be, I felt a sense of relief.

There was an old radiogram in a corner of the room. It needed to be repaired but several attempts to have it fixed had failed. I lifted the lid and found that the bunch of keys was inside it, on top of a record. I quickly put down the lid and came and sat in my chair. The bunch of keys looked like an insect, with seven or eight shiny legs. These unfamiliar insects can also be poisonous, I thought, and I shouldn't touch it. I was breathing rapidly. My eyes looked at each object in the room, turning from one to the other. I was aware of the shoe ashtray. I fidgeted with the newspaper and laid it aside. I saw a pencil. I twirled it around in my fingers a few times. I was feeling very hot. I untied my shoelaces and took off my shoes. They did not come off easily. When I bent down to take off my socks, I saw a fountain pen under the chair. I picked it up and put it on the table. I thought that if Baikunth didn't find the pen immediately he might think I'd stolen it. I heard Baikunth coming back. He had a sheaf of papers in his hand. He sat down at once. We kept sitting for a while. Neither of us moved.

'I found this pen under the chair.' My voice must have sounded different, for he did not hear me. My throat was parched.

'Did you say something?' Baikunth's attention was still on the papers when he said this.

'Nothing really. I found a bunch of keys while cleaning the house a few days ago. Old rusty keys,' I said casually. I don't know why I said it. Baikunth looked up at me as though he hadn't understood what I'd said. I looked away. Baikunth went back to the papers.

I'd barely stepped out of Kakka's house when I saw a black car approaching. It must be Kakka's car, I thought. I stood behind a tree so that Kakka wouldn't see me. But it wasn't his car. I continued walking, and as I did so I became aware that my right arm had gone stiff. I saw that my fist was closed tight. I opened my fist and found that I was holding the shoe ashtray in my palm which was damp with perspiration. I did not know how it came to be there. I returned to Kakka's bungalow and flung the ashtray inside the compound. I couldn't tell where it landed. My guess, not that it mattered, was that it landed near the garden tap. I walked home quickly. There was a dull pain in my stomach.

1964

old veranda

THE HOUSE IN RAIPUR that we moved into later has verandas that are more like rooms. It's hard to say why they aren't rooms, or what makes them verandas. One of them is called the old veranda. The house was built slowly and all at once. Since one of the verandas was the old veranda, the other became the new one. The old veranda of our house in Rajnandgaon is now in the house in Raipur. The pole star in Raipur is the same pole star that was in Rajnandgaon. Because there is the sky and the pole star, the homeless do not feel that they are homeless but that they live in the same one place under the same sky, which is the same everywhere. Even as a little boy in Rajnandgaon, I would think about the universe. However much you may learn about it afterwards, you never forget those early associations.

MY WIFE ASKS, 'DO you know where your brass lota is?'

'It's on the old veranda,' I tell her.

A friend who is sitting there asks, 'Isn't the house new?'

'It is,' I say.

'If you were building a new house, you should've built a new veranda as well.'

'The whole house is new. There used to be a quarry here. It's still around somewhere.'

'How many years ago was the house built?'

'About seventeen.'

'When will it become old?'

'Who's to say. When it's torn down.'

'I thought a house was torn down when it was old. Is the old veranda being torn down?'

'No, it's not. It's the same as it's always been. I don't remember it ever being any different.'

'I should be going. I've got to buy some wheat.'

'Where are you going to buy it?'

'Gole Bazaar.'

'You won't get new wheat. That only arrives in March.'

'I'll buy the old wheat. There's not a grain left to eat at home.'

'Do you like rotis?' I asked.

'Yes. But only fresh rotis.'

'Fresh ones?'

'Hot and fluffy. Not cold and stale.'

'I like fermented leftover rice,' I say.

'The rice may be fermented, but the grain it's made from is new,' he says.

'That man there carrying a pickaxe must have had some for breakfast,' he says, looking towards the road. Someone from the village is walking by with a pickaxe.

'So you've got this bag and you're going to buy wheat,' I say.

'Yes,' he says, 'to buy wheat.'

Then he leaves.

IF A BOY WANTS to become old, he should first add more years to his life. But what kept happening was that the person who was old was not getting old. The place of birth is where you're born. It's never about dying and being born again.

The old veranda in Rajnandgaon ran along the front of the house and the new one was built at right angles to it. The new veranda remained the new veranda even when the house was in ruins. When the foundation for the new veranda was being dug, they found a lot of worthless cowries, enough to fill several gunnysacks. Adjoining the old veranda was the birthing room, where even during the day it was dark inside. The only light came in from the door when it opened, the light like a sentry to keep the darkness from escaping. The darkness of the night remained in the room. In this way there were, in the room, two darknesses.

Whoever entered the birthing room took just two days to forget that there was anything like sunshine. Only the chirping of birds would have told them that it was morning. Had anyone else said that it was morning they wouldn't have believed it. They wouldn't even have believed Ajiya, though her words carried a lot of authority. Sunset happened only when you thought of sunset. If you thought of sunset at high noon it would be sunset. So much so that if you thought of midnight at midday it would be midnight. The birthing room was not a place where you thought of anything except the child who was about to be born.

If you closed your eyes, walked into the birthing room, and there opened them, for a long time it would seem that you hadn't remembered to do so. You could be deceived into thinking that your eyes had forgotten how to see. We stayed away from it irrespective of whether it was occupied or not, nor did we go anywhere near it when we played hide and seek.

INSIDE THE THRESHOLD OF the birthing room Amma kept her household gods. When someone went into labour the gods were shifted out, and after a month or so they were reinstated. Since ours was a large family this happened twice a year. Sometimes three times. If during the day the darkness did not emerge from the room even when the door was open, at night it would come out even when the door was shut.

Every birthday Amma would tie the year knot. She did not say 'birthday' but used the colloquial word. She'd take a cotton thread dyed with turmeric and tie a knot in it. In the knot she'd put a blade of new grass. We were three brothers, and for each of us there was a separate thread kept in a rusted tin. In the tin were also a yellow two-anna coin, a blackish one-anna bit, and two small betel nuts kept for prayer rituals. The money, even when it was really needed, was never touched. The tin box was kept inside a metal trunk in the birthing room. No one could go into the room without stubbing their toes on the trunk.

A day came when Amma stopped tying the year knots. It would sometimes happen that my knot would get tied on my older brother's thread or my younger brother's knot would be tied on mine. Going by the knots, my younger brother would become much younger than he was and my age would remain constant for several years. Amma would try and keep the record straight by adding more knots. If there were extra knots, she wouldn't allow them to be untied. If at the age of ten I had twelve knots in my thread, Amma let them be.

Amma would remember birthdays by associating them with events that happened around the same time. Krishna Talkies was inaugurated on the day I was born. The Talkies was built opposite our house. It was Rajnandgaon's first cinema hall and a big moment for the town. It's entirely possible that when, after five weeks, she came out of the birthing room, someone who was going to see a film took me along.

Krishna Talkies was owned by the Sapre brothers. They were my father's and uncle's friends, and they may all have had some business connections as well. The ushers knew us and we had free run of the place. Krishna Talkies was almost a part of our house. When one of us, to escape from the bath that we were being subjected to in the courtyard, slipped naked through the bars of the gate and ran into the Talkies, members of the family would go in search of the chowkidar to have the gate opened. Passers-by would stop to see what the fuss was about. The family would be afraid lest the boy reach the balcony, where he would be in danger of falling. A hawker selling rewri would arrive. He would put his hand through the bars and tempt the boy to come out and get the sweet, so he might catch hold of him. If you saw our house from Krishna Talkies, the house would have looked like an extension of it.

Women would only go to the cinema with other women, not with men. There was a separate entrance for them. The floor sloped towards the screen. It had rows of chairs followed by benches. There were toilets. The women's section took up the back of the hall, but only half of it. The other half had reserved seats. Urine from the women's toilet would spill out and after passing the first-class and second-class seats reach the front of the hall, where the third-class seats were. People would sit crouched, with their legs up on their seats. Few if any wore shoes. When they had to put their feet down they would first light a match to see whether the floor was wet.

One or two people had flashlights, and they usually sat in the first class or balcony. When the electricity went they would shine the flashlights so as to enable those sitting in the front of the hall to see. They would also shine them towards the screen. It gave people the feeling that the electricity had come back and the film would start soon. No one made a noise when the electricity went.

The viewers knew the names of those who were operating the projectors. They were greatly respected because they were the ones showing the films. They were considered to be particularly fortunate because they could watch films day and night. I was too young to understand what 'fortunate' meant, though I was fortunate too. I was old enough to know what sadness and happiness were, though sadness was easier to understand. It happened more often and perhaps that's why it was easier. The moments of happiness were few and far between.

The third class was right up in front, where the stage and the projection screen were. Children would lie down on the stage and watch the film from there. I'd often fall asleep. Phulesar Dai would then come looking for me and carry me home. If you knock on the door of the past, the past will come out. Some of it you'll recognize. It will have its age stamped on it. It's not very remarkable to say that I spent my childhood watching the world and watching cinema. Seen from the cinema's point of view, I was just another cinemagoer.

OURS WAS A FAMILY of four brothers living under one roof. The roof's shadow belonged to my youngest uncle, who was called Chachaji. He was called this at home and also outside, but wherever he was he largely kept to himself. Everyone was in awe of him. If he stepped out of the house more than he usually did, he came up against the world as if against a wall. He came up against it even when he was at home.

As happens in joint families, there would be quarrels. Guns would come out but were never fired. The women never quarrelled. Perhaps this was because of Amma, who continued to work quietly despite the chaos of marriages, births and deaths. I don't know how, but her quiet would have a calming effect on those who were grieving, and those who were full of joy would find the space around them expand to accommodate their laughter.

Amma would be up when it was still dark and would be the last to sleep. You could hear her in the kitchen putting things away, the clattering sounds like a lullaby for the night, sending it to sleep. Even the plants listened to her. As soon as it was twilight, the guava, the drumstick tree, and the tulsi in the courtyard would doze off, as would the soft grass in the corner and the two tomato plants that had appeared on the rubbish heap. The tall peepul tree to the east of the house would look in and, seeing the other plants asleep, go to sleep itself.

If she saw an ant in the fire crawling on a dung cake she would pull out the dung cake and save the ant. In the same way, she would save us from small everyday fires and hope that they wouldn't recur. The burn on her hand would not have healed before she burned herself again. Her daily routine was like a thread going through the different things she did, stringing them together. She never felt the needle's prick, but I did. In the papers I read about a man who was hospitalized and discovered to have hundreds of needles in his body. Was my condition similar to that man's?

Since Krishna Talkies was opposite our house, 'Cinema Line' was added to our address. At times when it seemed that the postal system had broken down, we were still certain of getting our letters. Such was our confidence that we believed that even if the postman forgot them somewhere, the letters would make their way on their own and we'd find them lying in the courtyard. Cinema Line got one more talkies when Rama Talkies opened near Manav Mandir Chowk. It was a short distance from our house and showed new releases. When we moved away from there our letters would be redirected to our new house. We thought that the letters had redirected themselves, or gone and found someone to redirect them.

IF WE WENT OUT for a stroll or to get something and turned left at Manav Mandir Chowk, we'd walk past the Brahmin Quarter and arrive at the fort. Hence the name Fort Quarter.

The quarter later became Digvijay College. I found it to be a strange place. For instance, the space between two classrooms to me appeared like a lane. There'd be a small house in it that had been rented out. The boys in the house would look like students, and the house like a classroom. My father looked like a teacher or someone who worked as a clerk there, when in fact he had nothing to do with it. When he went out shopping for vegetables, bag in hand, it would look like he was shopping for the college. The truth is that there is a mohalla in the precinct of the fort and the college was next to it.

And there was a grave there. The rumour was that every year it extended by a handspan. I kept thinking about what would happen if it were to grow so much as to get into someone's house. Around the fort were ponds that had shrunk to half or a quarter their size. Whenever I went to see Muktibodh I'd turn left at the Government Hospital or go right from the Chawkhadiya Quarter. On the way back I would take the path that ran from behind his house to Lalbagh and return via the hospital.

The first time that Muktibodh read me his poems it was late by the time I reached home. One of them had been a long poem about the sky. It had seemed as though a kite, tied to the string of time, were flying above the world and had been given plenty of line. Muktibodh handed me the spool after he'd finished reading. The poem had ended but it had not yet finished; it still hasn't. The light was fading by the time I left his place, and the street lights had come on. Soon it was dark. The people I met on the way were like the people one meets on the way. But I was seeing a lot more. I saw a man with two noses, a double nose. The road looked the same, but it had sunk a little. My feet, though, were firmly on the ground, the ground of practice and familiarity. It's not that I was stumbling but someone still asked, 'Are you all right?'

In those days Muktibodh lived in Basantpur. My elder brother had suggested that I show him my poems and that's how I'd first gone to see him. It was evening then too, and to me it seemed that it had turned dark only so that Muktibodh could come out with a lantern and dispel the darkness. He was wearing a pajama and a sleeveless banian.

Manav Mandir is where Babuji's house used to be. Babuji was my father's brother, the second oldest. He had moved into it while Grandfather was still alive. The house, he said, was built using a mixture of lime, jaggery, lentil paste and glue. But he fell on bad times and the house had to be sold. Later it burned down, and Manav Mandir Hotel was built in its place. The hotel did not have a door at the entrance, so it was always open. No one who arrived at the hotel had to go away because they found the entrance closed. If people didn't go there, it was simply because they'd decided to go elsewhere.

Once, Amma had given me some money to buy jalebis. Moti's shop was where we bought our sweetmeats and it was to the right of our house, on Bharat Mata Chowk. It had been there for ages. The Manav Mandir Hotel had not yet been built then. A dark-skinned man with shaggy curly hair made the jalebis. The karahi in which he was making them looked as if it were made of coal and not iron.

I asked him, 'So you didn't scrub the karahi today?'

'I haven't scrubbed it in fifteen years,' he said.

When I looked at his tangled curls and his oily perspiring face, I didn't have the heart to ask him, 'And what about a bath?'

But he said anyway, 'And I haven't bathed in eighteen.'

GRANDFATHER HAILED FROM JAGATPUR, a small village in Uttar Pradesh. He had come to Rajnandgaon, which was then a native state, and set up a grocery store opposite Moti's shop. The diwan of the state was a man called Kutubuddin who would routinely go around the market area to check if everything was in order. One day he stopped in front of Grandfather's new shop and made a few inquiries. Grandfather answered his questions, but he did not stand up and did not fold his hands in greeting. At least this is the story we heard from one of our uncles before he died. 'Do you sell liquor?' the diwan asked him. 'There's a lot of construction activity going on here,' he said. 'Why don't you become a contractor?' That's how Grandfather put some of his money into the new business.

Grandfather's family gradually got dispersed. Some of it settled in Rajnandgaon, the rest in nearby towns. If members of the family accidentally came face-to-face, they did not even need to pretend that they hadn't seen each other to go their separate ways. It was not as if they were parting for the first time. They were not meeting for the first time either. When they separated it was as if the separation had been there from the beginning and it had simply continued.

Krishna Talkies showed silent movies when it opened. I imagine that I'm sitting alone, in one of the five hundred seats in the third class, surrounded by quiet. It's a silent film. I have this distinct experience that I, like the film, think in scenes rather than in language, and that the screen on which the thinking takes place is white. I fall asleep in my seat and wake up when I hear a knock. The knock is not outside. It happens inside my mind. I then get up from my seat, still inside the mind. A man sitting behind me in the reserved section gets up and leaves. I don't know the man. He's wearing a blue shirt. I know blue. I know the blue of cloth. More than the cloth, I know the colour. The man's wearing a shirt made of blue. The man is wearing blue.

The sky was a bolt of blue cloth. Dina the tailor would call out our names and take our measurements. Because he stitched shirts from blue cloth, we associated him with the sky. Our uncle too got his clothes stitched by Dina. He always wore trousers made from white mercerized cotton manufactured by Rajnandgaon BNC Mills, where he worked as a manager. Dina was also the tailor to Raja Digvijay Das. One day our uncle called me and I went up using the inside stairs. Dina the tailor used the stairs that were on the outside. A bolt of white mercerized cotton had been rolled out on the clean red cement floor, and he measured me for a pair of trousers. Dina lived five or six houses away from us. He dressed like a man from the village but partnered my uncle in bridge at the club. On the day of the Akti festival, I would bring clay dolls for my sisters from Dina's house. Their clothes would be made from tailoring waste and their shiny eyes, their mouths, and ornaments for their hands and feet from silver foil.

The shirt the man in blue was wearing was made from a piece of sky. The day I wore my trousers made of mercerized cotton, my shirt was made from the sky too. I wore it tucked into my trousers and felt as though I were walking on a street that was high up in the air. I was barefoot as always. I took two steps and was over Gudakhu Line. From there, I was not scared when I saw the yard where condemned prisoners were hanged. The first thing that people see when they arrive in this town and come out of the station is Delhi Gate, built to commemorate Queen Victoria's visit to India. Above it was a door of strong gusts of wind that seemed to have been put there for me. I came out of this door wearing my trousers of mercerized cotton and strolled casually over Sadar and Bharkapara. There were others who were walking on air too. The man in a rickshaw coming from the station was returning to Rajnandgaon after many years.

'Back after a long time?' I asked him.

Travelling through the air at great speed was a bus bound for Rajnandgaon. The passengers and the bus driver were shouting with joy. There were no bars on the windows and the passengers waved their hands. Some were standing on the roof of the bus. A pigeon that had flown into it had got trapped inside, till a boy standing at the entrance released it.

It was evening, the time when birds return to their nests. All the birds of Rajnandgaon and all the people of Rajnandgaon were returning home. It was a returning crowd.

Since the road that passes through Delhi Gate was not wide enough, other roads were laid alongside it. The gate itself, built to commemorate Queen Victoria's visit, had largely been forgotten. I looked through memory's window and said to my mother, 'Amma, I'm going to school.' When I turned right from Manav Mandir and reached Urdu School, I realized that my mother had not heard me. So I went back, running all the way, faster than before. Amma was stoking the chulha by blowing through a piece of lead pipe and the kitchen was filled with smoke. I was panting when I said to her, 'Amma, I'm going to school.' 'Run along,' she replied, putting the pipe down. I was off again and got into the school compound through the place where the wall was broken. I went past the circular school building and reached the primary section. The morning bell had not rung yet.

ON THE IRON FENCING of the town hall, opposite the state high school, is the Latin saying A SOUND MIND IN A SOUND BODY. The words are repeated along the fence so many times that the mumbling is like a strong fence of its own, protecting the ruined garden and its few trees. Beneath one of them is an old man doing his daily exercises, in which he briefly stands up then sits down. Most of the time he's sitting.

MY NEPHEW WAS BORN in the birthing room the day Raja Sarvesvardas died. He works in the police. His mother, Bittan Jijji, talks a lot about the day when he was born, but as his retirement drew near he began to wonder if his age was not less than what was given in the official record. He wasn't looking forward to retirement. I suggested that he look in the gazetteer, where the date of Raja Sarvesvardas's death would surely be mentioned. If his actual age turned out to be less, I thought to myself, would it make any difference? Who would accept it?

After asking around, he discovered that the samadhis of the rajas were behind the Mata Devalaya temple and Raja Sarvesvardas's bore the date of his death.

He said to Bittan Jijji, 'Amma, I have to go to Rajnandgaon to find out the year of my birth.'

Bittan Jijji said, 'Didn't I tell you you were born on the day that Sarvesvardas died?'

My nephew said, 'You've said so many times. Today it'll be confirmed.'

Bittan Jijji said, 'There was so much confusion that day. The constabulary was all turned out in black.'

'Who told you?'

'Well, I knew it. Everyone did,' Bittan Jijji said.

'How come?'

'They just did. Wear your uniform when you go.'

'Why?'

'For no reason in particular.'

I said, 'You might also inquire at Krishna Talkies. Maybe you'll find the year of my birth written somewhere. I always forget to ask when I'm there.'

'A loyal subordinate, that's what I am,' the nephew said suddenly, just before leaving. 'Not the raja's, a subordinate of the people,' he said again, though no one had asked him.

'I am a viewer,' I said, closing my eyes. 'But not of the world. Of Krishna Talkies,' I added, though no one had asked me.

HE WAS POSTED IN Bhilai. It was hard to get a day off from work, but he got permission to go so long as he returned the same evening. He put on his uniform. Rajnandgaon was an hour away. An advantage of the uniform was that the bus conductor didn't accept the fare from him, nor did the bus stop anywhere to pick up passengers. He met an old acquaintance of his at the Rajnandgaon Bus Stand and bought him a cup of tea.

He immediately took a rickshaw to Mata Devalaya and from a distance paid his obeisance to the goddess. He kept the rickshaw waiting. People were beginning to stare at him, his policeman's clothes attracting their attention. He was in a hurry.

Some of the samadhis were in poor shape. One of them looked as if it had recently been cleaned. He moved to the next one. The writing on it was hidden under moss that had dried and turned black, so he could not read what it said. The grass growing beside the samadhi was dry. He pulled some out and scrubbed off the moss. His date of birth was engraved on the raja's samadhi: 18 September 1940.

2000

college

WE WERE IN THE last year of college. My younger brother was in the first year. All my free time went in going around the bazaar. It had become a habit. I quite enjoyed it. In college, in the evening, our games were hockey, kho-kho, chess, football and kabaddi. More than kho-kho, I liked to pick someone from the crowd and tail that person. There would always be people crossing the road in ones and twos. I much preferred watching them to watching kabaddi. To see a cow nosing its way into the vegetable market when the crowd was unaware of it was like watching a tamasha. You might see two cyclists collide, or a bag of flour spilt on the road. A lot could happen. I never attended college sports. I didn't like reading newspapers, though friends of mine were regular visitors to the Gandhi Reading Room. Walking in the bazaar was what I liked best.

We didn't need to shop every day. Twice a week we bought vegetables. Things like salt, lentils, rice, coriander and chillies were bought once a month. Watching other shoppers was more fun than being a shopper oneself. I could spend hours in the bazaar and still leave with the same amount of money I had when I arrived. It was easy to tell who the big spenders in the crowd were. Secretly following one of them around made you feel you'd seen everything there was to see. Returning from there, without having spent a paisa and with no compulsion to buy anything, gave me a sense of well-being. People who had to pass through the bazaar every day on their way to somewhere else would cross it quickly, while those who did not have the money to buy what they wanted to would save up to buy later. But none could escape the bazaar. Even beggars could become shoppers from the money they earned; people without any money could always borrow some, or they could steal. On the other hand, if you didn't have money you could be in the bazaar and the bazaar couldn't care less whether you died of hunger or for lack of medicines. Be that as it may, I still liked going there.

I would return home at night when the shops were closing and congratulate myself that I hadn't been overcharged. If I needed to step out again to get paan for my father, I would not go to Gange Guru's shop that was around the corner but cycle down to the bazaar. Not once in my experience did a shopkeeper make the mistake of returning more money than he should have, or I handed him more than I had to. Nor did any shopkeeper forget to take money from me. (A lot had to happen before there could be a bazaar. For there to be mangoes, there had to be trees. What was not grown locally had to come from outside. Apples, pineapples and litchis would arrive and be sold at once. Jewellery shops did good business. It was a matter of great joy that people would set out to buy okra and would return home after having bought okra. If arhar dal was out of stock they would get mung dal.)

My friend would tell me that in my first year of college I lacked confidence, though I'd improved afterwards. I don't know what else he'd have said if I'd flunked the exams even once. I was terrified of flunking. The college used to be an old fort. On three sides of it were ponds and on all four sides there were high walls. At the entrance was an enormous door made of thick planks of wood held together with iron bands. Because of its great height, even an open truck loaded to the top could pass through it. I never saw the door closed.

The windows of the classrooms that faced the pond were low enough for you to bend down and bail out the water. It's the sort of thing you might do sitting in a boat. There were four classrooms for first-year and two for fourth-year students. In the latter, the male students would sit with their legs dangling and pee in the water. The boys who chewed paan and tobacco positioned themselves near these windows.

The two third-year classrooms were situated far apart. In the interior of the building, between the classrooms, was a temple where it was always dark. There were also some tenants. They'd been there for decades. One of them was a clerk in the lower court and lived in three small rooms with his family, right next to the rooms where the postgraduate classes were held. The authorities tried very hard to get him to vacate. His son was in the same year as me. The soldiers' barracks had been converted into classrooms, the stable into a cycle stand. On one side was a mound on which were three ancient peepul trees, their aerial roots like crooked lines embedded in the wall. Under the trees was an enclosure, in which were stuck saffron flags, about twenty-five of them. There were stone idols, some standing and others lying on the ground. The faculty lived there as well. Outside the main entrance, huddled together, were several tea shops. There were other shops that sold paan or fritters. These tiny shops with tiled roofs were so close to the entrance that it looked as if they'd slowly shuffle their way into the college.

I remember that in my first year, during the rains, I felt as though the classes were being held in a boat. In the history class my attention would invariably be drawn to the floor. I would tap it with my foot and it would sound hollow. I was convinced that there was an underground chamber there. Ants would keep coming out from the stone floor, through joints that had to be filled with cement. Despite heavy monsoon rain, the water in the pond stayed below window level, though frogs would jump in and enter the classrooms. When it was quiet we could see herons sitting on the windows, facing the pond, and they would leave at the first hint of sound. The smell of fish was overpowering. The man in charge of cleaning the classroom, after he'd finished sweeping it, would put his hand into the water and pick up the withered flowers, the marigold garlands, the coconut husks, the banana leaves and the matchsticks that had swept up against the wall. Sometimes he would also find pencils, erasers and rulers floating in the water. However, because he was of low caste, he had once been driven away from the temple. After that, whenever he picked up the temple garbage he made sure to swear at the priest. When his son came down with smallpox and the smallpox goddess, so it was believed, was incarnated in the son, I had to go to his house and pay my obeisance to the goddess.

My tuition had been waived from the first year and I had to meet the principal to get the papers signed. While I was explaining my family circumstances to him, some of the plaster started falling from the wall and I could see the aerial root of the peepul hanging from it. The principal looked up, startled. He called out to the clerk, irritation in his voice, and pointed to the root. When the clerk tried to pull it out he ripped off more plaster till the root reached the end of the wall, which is when it finally broke. Only then did the principal sign the papers.

I liked studying finance and economics. The person who taught us economics dressed simply. He usually wore a white shirt and grey trousers. He was always leaning forward when he walked, half bent. If he had picked up something from the ground no one would even have noticed. His fingers were long and rough. On Sundays, he'd clean his house himself. He took a day off and painted his bicycle. We had an argument over savings once. He said that you need more buyers for any business to grow, because buyers try to spend as little as possible. I thought that if buyers spent less, it would affect sales and businesses would slowly collapse. We save so that we can buy what we need. But then what happens to the savings? Father would save some money but it would soon be spent. I could not understand how a man's money could grow if he bought expensive things and lived in a big house. The instructor said that if property or money was used to generate more wealth for only a few, inequality would increase. Not that I understood everything. The teacher never used the blackboard. In any case, when he was teaching I'd be staring at the moss covering the cracks in the walls. In the monsoon, from the corners of the blackboard, small plants with long, thin leaves would appear and the walls would be damp from floor to ceiling. In the evening, when I arrived for an extra class, I would see a couple of herons sitting on the desks. Their feet would leave wet marks and once in a while there'd be a half-eaten fish. The peepul would have countless herons sitting on it in the evening, and you could see their necks through the leaves. While a class was going on, an unsuspecting heron would appear in the door and quickly turn back and return to the tree. And immediately afterwards a latecomer would enter the class.

At the time of college elections but even otherwise, words like frog, tortoise, heron, alligator, fish, pond, water and fort were often heard. Because of the fort, the mohalla was called Fort Quarter. Another word that was often heard was raja. The neck feathers of the heron are extremely pretty, the kind that, along with diamonds, kings wear in their turbans. My house was in a part of town that for some reason was called Destitute Quarter. The rent was twenty-five rupees a month.

I'D MET PUTTAN ON the way. He didn't look too happy; from his shoulder hung an empty sling bag. Puttan was in the same class as my younger brother.

'Didn't you buy anything?' I'd asked him.

'I have to get sweet limes. They're five rupees a dozen, but Father said they were four.'

'Why don't you get a dozen bananas instead? They're a rupee a dozen.'

'I don't have to buy bananas. I have to get sweet limes and salt.'

'Salt is twenty paise a kilo.'

'White Tata salt is fifty-five paise a kilo,' Puttan had said.

I made Puttan buy the white Tata salt. I could have got him sweet limes at four rupees a dozen but they weren't fresh.

UTENSILS WERE ONLY BOUGHT occasionally. Sometimes spoons, sometimes katoris, and sometimes one thali. This was Father's job. On Dhanteras, when it was considered auspicious to buy utensils, we always bought something, even if it was a small katori. Most of our utensils I remembered from my childhood. I liked glass tumblers. They had to be used carefully and somehow seemed more hygienic. But my mother was always afraid that they might break. There was also a big brass tumbler. About six years ago my younger brother had dropped it in the privy. The jamadarin, whose job it was to empty the privy, had to be called to retrieve it. She was also made to clean the tumbler. It was then put in the fire for purification. The jamadarin wanted it for herself but Father had scolded her. Afterwards, she went around telling everyone that we brahmins drank water from a tumbler that had been caked with shit.

Father would buy utensils but look upon them as his savings. Whenever he needed money he would sell some. He never bought new utensils but old ones that were in good condition. He knew the shopkeeper. People would come and sell their old utensils which were practically new for less than half the price of the new ones. The shop was near a hospital, so it had a lot of customers. People from the villages would come to the hospital for treatment, but instead of money they would bring their utensils with them. The shopkeeper would have them cleaned and polished and sell them as new, doubling his profit. When cholera broke out or there was famine, the shopkeeper called it his 'season'. So much stuff would come in that he had to turn away the sellers. The villagers would plead with him and sell at a lower price.

Utensils of bell metal and brass would fetch a good price even if broken. After they'd sold their junk – strips of iron, broken stoves, rusted containers, bottles – both Father and Amma would look pleased. When the bargaining was being done, Amma would take up position behind the door, near the threshold. I was always embarrassed to witness the haggling. It had taken five or six years to collect that scrap; it hadn't been easy.

The biggest brass lota in the house had been kept aside for Father, for his exclusive use. After meals, he would remove his dentures and put them in the water that remained in the lota. My younger brother called the dentures our father's mouth. He would hold the dentures in his hands, open the hands in the shape of a jaw, and tell Amma to give Father a piece of the roti. The roti would drop in his palm. The dentures were made locally about a year ago. Father ever afterwards complained of pain in the gums. Being a brahmin, as part of his caste duties, he was frequently invited to eat at people's homes. Sometimes he'd forget to wear the dentures and Amma would nag me to go after him on my bicycle with them. Till I was in high school I would accompany him to these meals, as would my brother. Even when we were not keen to go with him, he would insist on taking us along. I had to restrain myself from eating my fill, but even so I could eat more than my father and brother. That pleased my father. When I refused the food that was being served, my father saw to it that I got another helping of churma and laddoo on my leaf plate. Father was in the habit of keeping an angocha over his shoulder. It also served as his sling bag. He earned a hundred and fifty rupees every month from the wood depot and was comfortably off.

We never needed to buy angochas. There were always half a dozen of them lying in the trunk, given to us on death ceremonies or death anniversaries. Many of the utensils were given as mementos. The big lota was given 'In memory of the late Ganga Din'. The other lota was 'In memory of Misra from Barahimpur'. There were fifteen pairs of wooden sandals in the house and a bundle of sacred threads. I'd stopped wearing a sacred thread. We had divided the utensils among ourselves and given them names. My thali was called 'Duniya na mane'; my younger brother's, 'Jhumroo'; Father's, 'Ghar ghar mein bhagwan'; and Amma's, 'Sant Sakhubai'. The names were those of old films, although the name that was inscribed on them said 'Late Bindadin Shukla' or something else. Even the old utensils that Father had bought were inscribed, for instance, 'Dhanaram Satnami Village Jora Thana Dharsiwa', or 'Bisahoo son of Dukaloo Village Chhokranala Thana Arang'. These old utensils from the village were practically new, whereas those that came from the city were in poor shape. Utensils that had been bought just two days ago were taken back by the shopkeeper, but he only gave half price for them.

IN THE PLAY FOR the annual function my friend had the role of an old man. They had to use a lot of make-up to make him look the part. He was fair-complexioned, and if he hadn't been so tall he could easily have played the girl's role. In the play, she'd done her matriculation but could not continue with her education because her father had died suddenly. Luckily, she married a rich man and lived happily ever after. Had my friend not been so thin he could have played the role of the district magistrate's son, and had he not been so fair and good-looking he could have played the servant. The teachers wanted him in the play at any cost. My younger brother was not involved in it at all. I did not mind that. (Except for a few, most boys did not have anything to do with the play. Boys good at chemistry were also good at physics; there were many who failed. Those who did well were often from comfortably off families. Hukumchand Kothari, who always stood first, was the son of a rice mill owner.)

The servant was played by a boy in the second year. He was a bit of a rogue and had agreed to the part quite readily. We had discouraged him from accepting it, but he said it didn't matter. He knew that he could thrash the boy whose servant he was in the play anytime he wanted. This was true. He and I were together in the first year. If one day he showed us dirty pictures, the next day most of the women in the pictures looked pregnant to us, and his moustaches upturned with pride.

My younger brother would say to Amma, 'Why doesn't Father do the old man's role in the play? He's the right age, and anyway he sits around at home making some powder or other, if not triphala for digestion then something for the teeth. He has a fat nose, which we've inherited. He has long nails and so do we. You can hardly call him a representative of old money. He eats paan but only after pounding it in a mortar and pestle. His cannot have roasted gram unless it's been turned into flour. When he dies he'll leave behind his dentures. The upper one for my elder brother and the lower one for me.'

I said to Father, 'I will pass the college exams this year. If you put in a word, Tiwariji is sure to give me a job in the municipality.' Father was on good terms with its secretary, Baldev Prasad Tiwari. The advantage of this was that the privy and drain were cleaned both morning and evening. Because my Father had complained, the jamadarin had twice been replaced.

The minute the jamadarin saw me she would put down her basket and broom and politely greet me with folded hands. When I greeted my teachers or Baldev Prasad Tiwari, I would not put down my book or my sling bag. When I was still a child, the neighbourhood barber would deliberately wish me by saying, 'I touch your feet,' and I would wish him similarly, 'I touch your feet.' The people sitting around would burst out laughing. Only later did Father explain to me that if someone says 'I touch your feet' in greeting, the proper answer is 'My blessings' or 'May you be happy'.

Amma would give the jamadarin some dry puris and rotis, but leave them for her on the ground. If there was something to be done around the house in which there was fear of caste pollution, Amma would wear kosa silk. Father believed that pollution does not affect kosa silk, wool, gold or money.

I would argue with Father and say, 'These are all expensive things. Name a few that everyone can afford.' When I said to him, 'So it's only the poor who pollute,' he had got irritated and said, 'We are poor too.'

'We're bees biswa brahmins, the highest category, and will always remain so, poor or not,' my younger brother had said.

Irritated by all this, I would bathe once in fifteen days even in summer, and then too only after Amma had screamed at me. And in winter I would go without a bath for months. Amma would call me a mleccha, a barbarian.

Father knew a brahmin the very thought of whom made me uncomfortable. It would always be me who was sent to him when we needed to borrow money.

'Father has asked to borrow fifty rupees.'

'Are you wearing your sacred thread?'

'No.'

'Go and bathe first, wear your sacred thread, and then come back for the money.' Father would not go himself out of fear, which meant that I had to bathe and wear the thread and go back after an hour. If the money was not returned in time the brahmin would become violent. He was always ready with a wise saw, 'Losers know no shame', 'You have to die first to see heaven', 'Better miser than god, at least you get an answer', 'A son who's got his share of the property is as good as a neighbour', and many others.

For the past year there had been a demand for my horoscope. The request always came on a reply-paid postcard. Father or my younger brother would copy the horoscope on the card. In his reply, Father would always put in one word,

'Commitment', by which he meant dowry. In his enthusiasm to show me to my prospective in-laws, he would once in a while turn up in college with them. It did not take me long to recognize the prospective in-laws. They would be carrying a sling bag which had one durrie, a change of clothes and, right on top, a lota. Father had made it known that I would be getting a job as soon as I graduated. Those who doubted the assurance were taken to meet Baldev Prasad Tiwari, while those whose proposals were rejected were not replied to at all and the reply-paid card was used to write to my uncle in Sikathiyapur. The uncle would never write back, afraid that Father would turn up at his house and claim his five bighas of land. Every year Father would plan a trip but never managed to put together the money for it. The whole family had been to Sikathiyapur only once and that was twenty years ago, when I was six months old.

The jamadarin would keep asking Amma when I'd get married. She'd been promised a sari when I did. She never had money for anything and even a five-paisa coin made her a buyer. She would come to know from Amma the houses where Father was invited for a ceremonial feast. These were occasions when many guests could be expected and a lot of food left over. The jamadarin would sit beside the garbage dump and wait. These dumps had a pecking order. In the one where the rubbish thrown out by Nathani went, people like us could find many things that we could use. Nathani was a wealthy merchant and we would never have thrown the things that he did. If the jamadarin found something in the dump where our rubbish went, I was not surprised. I always wondered if the jamadarin had any rubbish of her own. When I was a young boy, in the garbage dump behind the lower courts I would find carbon paper, erasers, pencils, nib holders, nibs, small packets of ink powder, blank sheets of paper, postage stamps and large envelopes. What astonished me most about the jamadarin was that she could carry on her head a basket smeared with ash and full of excrement, while tucked in her waist would be a pouch containing her rotis.

BECAUSE OF THE ANNUAL function, there was a lot of activity in the hostel till late at night. The whole place was lit up. The hostel consisted of a row of twenty-five rooms, many of them unoccupied. A group of boys in their underclothes were massaging their gums with tobacco paste, getting ready for bed. The language teacher was standing on the veranda. He was short, which is probably why he looked muscular. He was in charge of dramatics and sports. There was a crowd of boys around him and they were having an argument. As the argument grew more heated the boys who had been massaging their gums joined in. Then it became a free-for-all. The moment before it started was poised in the same way that the second hand of a clock is poised before it strikes twelve. The teacher had come down from the veranda and stood near the field. The boys and the teacher were as one body that kept moving forward and backward. The crowd was now at a little distance from the veranda. Small groups of boys who had broken from the crowd stood around in their underclothes, still massaging their gums, then sat down in a row on the edge of the veranda.

In the meantime, eight boys in the group had acquired hockey sticks and a cricket bat. One boy had a football. He lived near the main mosque. The boys with hockey sticks were from the Brahmin Quarter. Those who were not carrying anything were from the kabaddi and kho-kho teams. The teacher had angrily snatched the ball and had run out towards the field. There was pandemonium. It was dark and you could hardly see the green bushes at the edge of the field. The teacher had thrown the ball towards the bushes. The ball made a distinctive sound – thump thump thump – as it hit the ground. The crowd had split and the students were running in all directions. Some of the boys were from poor backgrounds, but at night it was hard to recognize them. Apart from Muslims and brahmins, there were boys from other castes as well. The teacher would have taken out the whistle from his pocket and then he must have gone home.

(Someone kept blowing the whistle and the whistle was meant for him, so the teacher would have thought, for he kept committing one foul after another, and in the morning that was still to come he would have searched for his glasses. When the sun had risen and he could see clearly, it was as though he'd been wearing them. Not that his eyes were weak. He would have noticed the torn book in the library; a marble would have looked as big as a football to him. Everywhere the air was solid and there was no movement. At the point till where the eye could see in the dark was my football.

I was inside the football, being kicked around. Why do such thoughts come to me?)

Usually he'd be seen in the sports room. The room was small and filled with sports equipment, most of it broken. Next to his table were two gymnast's clubs. On the table was a jumble of papers. They were held down by a cricket ball in the same way that his heavy, round head was a paperweight, keeping his disorganized body in place. He expected everyone to have the sporting spirit. When in deep thought he would have his head in his hands and look as if he was trying to dodge a football coming at him. His head would remain in the same position. Anything could happen. Usually there was a problem that had to be dealt with, not that there was really a problem.

Many people had come for the college play. My father did not come, nor did my friend's father. My friend's father had a small shop that sold scented chewing tobacco. My friend would chew it all the time. The play ended at around one in the morning. The venue was a large hall. In the front row was Baldev Prasad Tiwari, the secretary of the municipal corporation. From time to time I would look in his direction. I felt happy to see him laugh, but he left early. After the play ended we found the chowkidar asleep on a durrie under the makeshift stage. Two boys from the mohalla were dozing there too.

My friend had acted well, better than anyone else. It did not take more than five minutes for the hall to empty out. A few people had flashlights. Those who found themselves without one joined the ones who did. It was dark and the ground was uneven. Some of those who were walking alongside the people with flashlights could have been their friends and took advantage of it. The others may simply have attached themselves to the group. Baldev Prasad Tiwari had left with his friends in a car. The magistrate's car carried only him. The flashlight was not a car that only a few could take advantage of. The road belonged to everyone. So long as there was a crowd, one-thirty in the morning did not seem like one-thirty in the morning. Then suddenly it was two o'clock. The bright lights had been turned off. Only the fairy lights were left burning.

There were some sounds coming from behind the stage. The students were getting out of their costumes and there were three teachers having a cup of tea with the principal. The boy who had played the servant was sitting in a corner by himself and had not changed his clothes. He was smoking a bidi. The principal put down his cup of tea, got up, and hit the boy with his fist. He snatched the bidi from his mouth and threw it out of the window that was facing the pond. It struck me that you needed a whole pond to put out one bidi. In the play he was being a little more obsequious than necessary. The servant in the play was both lazy and a thief. He was not paid on time. His salary was twelve rupees a month. The play had ended but the atmosphere was still that of a play. If there were to be a servant's role again in the annual play, the same boy would be chosen.

After the principal left, the boy who had played the role of the girl emerged from behind the curtain and walked away quickly. A little later, one of the teachers also left. He was walking behind the boy. My friend was standing beside a large wooden box in which the costumes were being put. He said in a tired voice, 'I can't find my shoes.' He had not removed his make-up. We were both in a hurry to get home. I said, 'You are an old man who cannot find his shoes.' We took permission from the teachers and pushed off.

I wanted to walk fast and reach home as quickly as possible, but my friend was in a mood to have some fun. He said, 'The shops shut by eight-thirty but the bustle on the roads continues for a few hours afterwards.'

'Shops should remain open all night,' I said, swinging my empty sling bag in the dark. We had now come on to the road. Standing in front of a new house that looked empty, I said loudly, 'This house is not for sale.'

'Even if it was,' my friend said, 'how would we have taken it home in your bag?'

'You already have a house. Why do you need another?' I said to him. I was irritated.

When we reached the bazaar, my friend said, 'I am an old man and need support.' I smiled and played along. To give him support, I put my left hand on his right shoulder. 'You look like your father,' I said. At which he started coughing as though he was asthmatic. It was all part of the tomfoolery. Hearing him cough, about fifty dogs that hung around the Meat Market started barking. That shut my friend up. He was scared.

Right next to us was a neem tree. In the dark, the neem tree did not look like a real neem tree. It looked like some other tree dressed up like a neem. The same was the case with the other trees. Then we came to the magistrate's bungalow.

His car was parked outside. The veranda light was on. There was nothing there to suggest that the magistrate had come to the play. The house looked like a house that had been dressed up to look like a magistrate's bungalow. The scene looked as though it was a stage set.

'Your shop does good business,' I said.

'Why are you talking about things that were not in the play?'

Someone called out to us from behind. It was one of the teachers. He had a flashlight and was walking towards us.

'Shyam Lal Gupta, you are still wearing your costume,' he said, flashing the light in our faces. 'You know that I'm responsible for it and for the stage props.'

'I've lost my shoes. Who's responsible for them?'

'You can box my ears twice, if that's any help,' the teacher mumbled angrily and walked away.

There was a large field. It was pitch dark. The darkness seemed to have acquired layers that rose to a great height and extended in all directions. Through familiarity and with a little guesswork I could tell where the ground was. I wanted to take the footpath and cross the field with the same familiarity.

Next to the field was a primary school. There was a hill with a big tamarind tree. At the bottom of the hill was an idgah. A lane behind the school went past the idgah and a hospital. There was a bidi workshop in this lane, Randhir Bidi Factory. The locality around the factory was called Bharkapara. The mohalla was filthy. Most of the people who lived there belonged to the mahar caste. They worked in the bidi factory. The whole family, including the women and children, would sway their bodies backward and forward as to a rhythm when they rolled the bidis. It was the people from this mohalla who went behind the hill to defecate in the open, and that's where the stench came from. A small office in the mohalla had a red flag fluttering over it. Processions would occasionally emerge from the office, everyone shouting slogans at the top of their voices. Eight- or ten-year-olds were quick at rolling bidis. They had dropped out of school after class four and started to work in order to earn money.

'If you don't study, what will you do? Roll bidis?' Father would say when he scolded us for neglecting our studies. Not a single boy from this mohalla had been to college. Only a few days ago, my younger brother had told Father that he had had enough education and wanted to get a job. Father had said, 'Go and join the bidi factory then.' I'd come to realize that unless the entire family worked at making bidis, it would not have enough to eat. Father did not like the idea that we should work while still in college. He said that in respectable homes a person earns to make a better life for his children. You should take up a job only after graduation, even if it means eating only one meal a day. But even after graduation, I would think to myself, two meals a day was just about all you could expect.

In primary school, we would often play in that field. In one of the games, we kept a piece of paper on the ground in the belief that if it was touched by a pariah kite's shadow it would turn into a rupee note. We'd keep pieces of paper in our pockets and wait for the kite. The kite would be wheeling in the sky. Its shadow would move rapidly over the uneven ground and climb up the hill. Holding a scrap of paper and crouching low, we'd chase the kite's shadow. As soon as we got the chance, we'd try and place the piece of paper inside it but the shadow would already have moved away. The scrap of paper would fly about in the breeze. We wasted many pages of our exercise books doing this, for we never had any other paper available. I could easily climb up the tamarind tree. When boys were up on the tree and felt like peeing, they'd pee from there. I'd pee either before climbing the tree or would come down and do so.

'Can you see the kite flying up there?' I asked.

'How can I see in the dark?'

'Do you have some spare paper?'

'I have a fountain pen.'

'It's no good keeping a fountain pen in the kite's shadow. Darkness is the shadow of a large kite.'

I found a small piece of paper in my pocket. It was a receipt for some things I'd bought. We put the piece of paper on the ground and bent down to look at it. Then my friend picked up the piece of paper and put it in his pocket. But I snatched it back from him. A piece of paper is still a piece of paper.

ON TUESDAYS, WHEN THE shops were closed, I studied till late. I resented their being closed. There was no separate room or a quiet place at home to study. I remembered the large wooden box at the college. It was large enough for two people to sit comfortably inside. Our house was a little like that box. As soon as evening fell there would be a smell, as of something burning. The whole mohalla had the same smell.

I asked Amma about it. She said it was of flaxseed oil. We used groundnut oil for cooking. It was expensive. When my exams approached, I'd stop doing the shopping and Father would take over from me. I was always afraid that he'd get ripped off. Rising prices were another source of anxiety.

Amma too had a wooden box. It had belonged to Ajiya and had several small compartments in which were kept loose change, betel nuts for prayer rituals, a religious book about the goddess Durga, and two cotton threads dyed with turmeric. One was for me and the other for my brother. Every year on our birthdays Amma would tie a knot in them. She was in the habit of eating opium. With the help of some finely filtered ash, she'd make pellets the size of coriander seeds from a sticky lump of opium, and stash them away to eat later. Amma looked very old. She had a wooden comb that she would run through her hair. She'd collect the hair that came away in the comb and make a string from it. She'd use it to tie her hair. I joked with her that if she collected the entire family's hair, she could knit a sweater for me. I offered to have my head shaved and give her the hair so that she could knit me a cap. Balls of tangled hair, the string that she made from it, the wooden comb and her small casket of opium were kept inside the trunk. The trunk was locked and the key hung from a string round her neck.

My friend had come to my place on Tuesday so that we could study together. If we drew up a schedule and followed it, we managed to get some work done. My friend had all the books that we needed. He was cleverer than me. We spread out a bamboo mat on the veranda and sat down to study. My brother and I were wearing similar clothes, a blue shirt and khaki shorts. We intended to concentrate on our studies. My friend had bad breath.

'Your mouth smells real bad when you don't chew scented tobacco,' I said.

'No it doesn't.' He brought his mouth close to my nose. 'Ha!' he said, and exhaled. I pushed him away. My younger brother held him by his hands and I went 'Ha! Ha! Ha!' at him in retaliation. Father arrived just then. He had a bottle of groundnut oil in his right hand and in his left he was holding his bunched up dhoti. He took off his chappals near the door and was about to go in.

'Namaste,' my friend greeted him.

'How come you found a shop that was open on Tuesday?' I asked a little anxiously.

'There's one in Nayapara that stays open.'

'The fellow must have overcharged you,' I muttered.

'We were out of oil,' Father said.

'The vegetable couldn't be cooked without oil. And you wouldn't have eaten without the vegetable,' said Amma.

'I won't now have the vegetable even if you cook it,' my younger brother said.

'It was nine rupees a kilo. It's clean oil,' Father said.

'If you'd waited for a day I would have got it for eight rupees a kilo.'

'Be quiet,' Father shouted and went in. Amma followed him.

'Do you know where the bottle of oil is?' I asked my friend.

'How would I know? Must be in the kitchen.'

'Yes, he must have hung it from a peg there,' said my younger brother.

There came the sound of digging in the courtyard.

'Father is burying the bottle of oil,' said my younger brother.

'Come, let's go and see,' said my friend.

'Why would he bury it? The bottle doesn't have a cap. Mud will get into it,' I said.

When the three of us entered, Father was shaking out some gunny sacks. He spread out one of them and sat down near Amma.

'The price of old bell metal is now nineteen and a half rupees a kilo,' Father said to Amma.

'What about new bell metal?' I asked.

'That's forty rupees a kilo. Old brass is touching fifteen.'

'Why don't we sell the thali?' I said to Father. 'It weighs two kilos. We have no use for it.'

'It came in your mother's trousseau.'

'The bicycle tyres and tubes need to be changed,' my younger brother said. There was no sign of the bottle of oil.

'Where's the oil? I'll go and return it.'

'Let it be.' Father had started slicing the potatoes.

Amma had covered herself with an unwashed sari and was lying in a corner. Only her feet were visible. There were silver ringlets on her thin wrinkled toes and a double-band ring on the toe next to the big toe.

'Amma! Get up!' I shouted.

'Leave her alone,' Father said.

'Where is the ringlet from one of your toes? It's missing,' said my younger brother.

Amma got up hurriedly, but when she saw the commotion she lay down again.

'You've gone mad,' said Father irritably.

'The bottle of oil is up there on a peg,' said my friend, pointing to it. There was an empty sling bag hanging next to it. My father had stopped slicing the potatoes and the three of us had come out. I had the bottle in my hand.

'You go and study,' I said to my younger brother.

'I want to come too,' he said. He wanted to be the one holding the bottle.

'No,' I said angrily. When he stretched out a hand to take the bottle, I held his hair with my left hand and pushed him aside. My younger brother went back. Studies too were important after all. I had not changed my clothes and was wearing my new khaki shorts. I thought the shopkeeper would not be impressed by my shorts and refuse to take back the oil.

That's what happened. The shopkeeper did not take back the oil. I walked further on and came to the railway tracks. My friend had gone home. At a little distance from the tracks were two men sitting under a shisham tree. They looked to be fathers.

'Aren't you panditji's son?' one them shouted out to me.

'Yes,' I said.

'Have you had a quarrel at home that you've come here? The exams haven't yet begun,' he yelled out to me again.

'No, I haven't had a quarrel,' I said, turning towards him.

'Then what are you doing here? Go home. It's time for the train to come.'

He saw the bottle when I turned to go back.

'What's in the bottle?'

'It's groundnut oil.'

They laughed.

Some of the oil had got spilt on the way. The day the results came out, fathers were worried about their sons. A couple of years ago a boy who had failed the exam had thrown himself in front of a train. On the day of the results, fathers would keep an eye on the railway tracks and on the ponds and wells. The police too would be there. The windows of the college that opened on to the pond would be closed. Inwardly, I cursed myself for having gone near the tracks.

I'd told Father that I was not ready for marriage. My voice had become gruff. I could shout down anyone. I'd been in several scuffles with my friend. My trips to the bazaar had become infrequent. We didn't need to buy much anyway. I'd started going to the Bharkapara Reading Room in the evenings. I looked on the bazaar as if it was my enemy. I'd begun to understand things like dishonesty, hoarding, profiteering. The finance and economics teachers had been dismissed from college.

1975

Vinod Kumar Shukla is a poet and novelist from Raipur, Chhattisgarh. In 1999, Shukla received the Sahitya Akademi Award for his novel, *Deewar Mein Ek Khidki Rehti Thi*. In 2023, he was awarded the PEN/Nabokov Award for Achievement in International Literature.

Arvind Krishna Mehrotra is the translator of *The Absent Traveller: Prakrit Love Poetry*, *Songs of Kabir* and *Treasurer of Piggy Banks*, a selection of Vinod Kumar Shukla's poems.

Sara Rai has translated *The Golden Waist-Chain* and *Premchand's Kazaki and Other Marvellous Tales*. Her memoir, *Raw Umber*, won the Tata Literature Live! Book of the Year Award 2023 for non-fiction.

HARPERPERENNIAL

Harper Perennial presents special editions of its finest books in translation

Apradhini
Shivani
Translated from the Hindi by Ira Pande

Avasthe
U.R. Ananthamurthy
Translated from the Kannada by Narayan Hegde

Blue Is Like Blue
Vinod Kumar Shukla
Translated from the Hindi by Arvind Krishna Mehrotra and Sara Rai

Diary of a Malayali Madman
N. Prabhakaran
Translated from the Malayalam by Jayasree Kalathil

Farewell, Mahatma
Devibharathi
Translated from the Tamil by N. Kalyan Raman

The Golden Gandhi Statue from America
Subimal Misra
Translated from the Bengali by V. Ramaswamy

A Name for Every Leaf
Ashok Vajpeyi
Translated from the Hindi by Rahul Soni

Moustache
S. Hareesh
Translated from the Malayalam by Jayasree Kalathil

Seven Sixes Are Forty-Three
Kiran Nagarkar
Translated from the Marathi by Shubha Slee

Shameless
Taslima Nasreen
Translated from the Bengali by Arunava Sinha

HARPERPERENNIAL

Age of Frenzy
Mahabaleshwar Sail
Translated from the Konkani by Vidya Pai

A Life Incomplete
Nanak Singh
Translated from the Punjabi by Navdeep Suri

Mohanaswamy
Vasudhendra
Translated from the Kannada by Rashmi Terdal

The Music of Solitude
Krishna Sobti
Translated from the Hindi by Vasudha Dalmia

No Presents Please
Jayant Kaikini
Translated from the Kannada by Tejaswini Niranjana

A Preface to Man
Subhash Chandran
Translated from the Malayalam by Fathima E.V.

The Secret Garland
Andal
Translated from the Tamil by Archana Venkatesan

Shala
Milind Bokil
Translated from the Marathi by Vikrant Pande

The Weary Generations
Abdullah Hussein
Translated from the Urdu by the author

Written in Tears
Arupa Patangia Kalita
Translated from the Assamese by Ranjita Biswas

HARPERPERENNIAL

Bhima
M.T. Vasudevan Nair
Translated from the Malayalam by Gita Krishnankutty

Chemmeen
Thakazhi Sivasankara Pillai
Translated from the Malayalam by Anita Nair

Ghachar Ghochar
Vivek Shanbhag
Translated from the Kannada by Srinath Perur

Hindutva or Hind Swaraj
U.R. Ananthamurthy
Translated from the Kannada by Keerti Ramachandra and Vivek Shanbhag

The Liberation of Sita
Volga
Translated from the Telugu by T. Vijay Kumar and C. Vijayasree

A Life Misspent
Suryakant Tripathi Nirala
Translated from the Hindi by Satti Khanna

The Sea Lies Ahead
Intizar Husain
Translated from the Urdu by Rakhshanda Jalil

Selected Poems
Joy Goswami
Translated from the Bengali by Sampurna Chattarji

Wild Animals Prohibited
Subimal Misra
Translated from the Bengali by V. Ramaswamy

Wild Words
Malathi Maithri, Salma, Kutti Revathi and Sukirtharani
Translated from the Tamil by Lakshmi Holmström

HarperCollins *Publishers* India

At HarperCollins India, we believe in telling the best stories and finding the widest readership for our books in every format possible. We started publishing in 1992; a great deal has changed since then, but what has remained constant is the passion with which our authors write their books, the love with which readers receive them, and the sheer joy and excitement that we as publishers feel in being a part of the publishing process.

Over the years, we've had the pleasure of publishing some of the finest writing from the subcontinent and around the world, including several award-winning titles and some of the biggest bestsellers in India's publishing history. But nothing has meant more to us than the fact that millions of people have read the books we published, and that somewhere, a book of ours might have made a difference.

As we look to the future, we go back to that one word—a word which has been a driving force for us all these years.

Read.

Harper Collins
4th
HARPER PERENNIAL
HARPER BUSINESS
HARPER BLACK
हार्पर हिन्दी
HarperCollins *Children'sBooks*
HARPER DESIGN
HARPER VANTAGE
Harper Sport

